"I'll listen, Tucker," Ginny whispered, covering his hand on the table with hers.

"Whatever you have to say, I'll listen."

Tucker threaded his fingers through hers, his eyes steady on her face. Something fluttered through his brown gaze, but it was gone as quickly as it came. He raked a hand through his dark hair, huffed in a great quantity of air, then exhaled in it one whoosh.

"I counted on that," Tucker admitted quietly. "I came back because I need you to help me, Gin." His words rebounded around the kitchen with a desperate plea, even though his voice had dropped to a deadly, whisper-soft calm.

Ginny stared. "Help you do what?"

"Help me figure out what's wrong. I need a way to get God to listen to me, to hear me. I need you to explain how I can find God."

Ginny gulped, shocked by the admittance, stunned by the truth she saw reflected in his eyes.

Books by Lois Richer

Love Inspired

A Will and a Wedding #8
†*Faithfully Yours* #15
†*A Hopeful Heart* #23
†*Sweet Charity* #32
A Home, a Heart, a Husband #50
This Child of Mine #59
Baby on the Way #73
Daddy on the Way #79
Wedding on the Way #85
‡*Mother's Day Miracle* #101
‡*His Answered Prayer* #115
‡*Blessed Baby* #152
Tucker's Bride #182

†Faith, Hope & Charity
*Brides of the Seasons
‡If Wishes Were Weddings

LOIS RICHER

lives in a small Canadian prairie town with her husband, who, she says, is a "wanna-be farmer." She began writing in self-defense, as a way to escape. She says, "Come spring, tomato plants take over my flower beds, no matter how many I 'accidentally' pull up or 'prune.' By summer I'm fielding phone calls from neighbors who don't need tomatoes this fall. Come September, no one visits us and anyone who gallantly offers to take a box invariably ends up with six. I have more recipes with tomatoes than with chocolate. Thank goodness for writing! Imaginary people with imaginary gardens are much easier to deal with!"

Please feel free to contact Lois at: Box 639, Nipawin, Saskatchewan, S0E 1E0 Canada.

Tucker's Bride
Lois Richer

Love Inspired®

Published by Steeple Hill Books™

STEEPLE HILL BOOKS

Steeple
Hill™

ISBN 0-373-87189-9

TUCKER'S BRIDE

Copyright © 2002 by Lois Richer

Visit us at www.steeplehill.com

Printed in U.S.A.

But those who hope in the Lord
will renew their strength. They will soar on wings
like eagles; they will run and not grow weary,
they will walk and not be faint.

—*Isaiah* 40:31

This book is dedicated to Aven Paetkau and Lyn Cote, true friends who so graciously support me through all the rough empty spots in my life. You always bring me joy and comfort. Bless you.

Chapter One

Two things hit Tucker Townsend squarely between the eyes on his first evening back in Montana.

First, after seven years, Ginny Brown was more beautiful than he remembered. And second, even Jubilee Junction, the place he'd once thought stoically immune to change, had probably been transformed from the homey little haven of his youth.

And why not? Nothing else in his life had stayed the same.

Still, hope burned inside, refusing to be dampened—hope that with the rest of his life in upheaval, Ginny and the Junction would be there, rock solid as always. He'd needed to believe that, for his own self-preservation. Over the past days and weeks, he'd clung to his memories of Ginny and the sleepy little town like a kid clings to Santa Claus.

Please God, let this be the place I find answers.

"Hey, Tuck! I wondered when you'd get here. Your phone calls are always too short." Coach Bains whacked him on the back hard enough to topple an oak tree. The wrinkled face beamed with delight. "I knew you'd come here first."

The little white church—his sanctuary. Back in the old days, hadn't he always run here first when he was in trouble? Looking for a miracle, no doubt. Tucker winced at the foolishness of that. There were no miracles, not for him.

"You're just in time to celebrate."

Tucker could see that. At First Avenue Church, the fellowship hall hummed with vibrant displays of spring daffodils and rich blue hyacinths. There were baskets crammed full of the wild lilac crocus flowers he remembered from springtimes past. The verdant forest green of ferns and newly budded leaves arranged in the center of each table only added to the riot of color.

But all of this bounty took second place to the paper wedding bells dangling over Ginny Brown's curly head.

"What's up, Coach?" Tucker forced his eyes off Ginny and the masculine arm tossed so carelessly behind her shoulders.

"Bridal shower."

Tucker swallowed. Hard. So Ginny *was* getting married, the bells weren't an illusion his damaged eye had conjured up. He should be happy for her. So why did he suddenly feel as if he'd been abandoned?

Because he desperately needed her help.

Tucker quashed that thought immediately. He had no right to ask her. None. She owed him nothing, no explanations, no justification for her choices, nothing at all. He'd forfeited everything while he chased his dream.

Coach leaned closer. His voice dropped a decibel.

"Nice things, these showers. Everybody gets to celebrate before all the hoity-toity of the wedding. Don't have to wear a suit here, either." Coach's merry blue eyes winked with fun.

"You own a suit?" Tucker tore his eyes away from Ginny long enough to blink at the old man.

"Yep. Wear it once, maybe twice every year. I suspect the wife'll dig it out when this shindig happens, too."

"And when might that be?" Tucker swallowed again, his eyes moving to Ginny and the man who sprawled on the chair next to hers.

Riley Cantrel. Tucker should have guessed. Riley had always planned his life down to the nth degree. He probably had lists of pros and cons when it came to Ginny, though there couldn't be many cons. Ginny would make a great wife. But not for Tucker. Never for him.

"I guess it's time she got married." He pretended a nonchalance he absolutely did *not* feel.

"Way past time, if you ask me. All this thinking and making up problems where there aren't any. In my time we just got married. Then we handled the problems. Made life a whole lot easier." Coach snorted his indignation.

"She's been going with him for that long?" Tucker mocked himself. He'd been a fool to run back here, tail between his legs. What had made him think Ginny would even speak to him after seven long years?

"What's the matter, your other eye doesn't work, either?" Coach jerked his thumb forward and to the left. "They must have taken a hunk of your brain out if you don't remember how long those two have been a couple."

"I guess I forgot." Tucker frowned as he watched Ginny tilt her head to whisper something in Riley's ear.

Coach poked him in the ribs, face perplexed.

"You forgot Drusilla Andrews and Rob Lassiter have been canoodling in corners since tenth grade? You better see a doctor, son. You're sicker than I thought."

Tucker's breath whooshed out of his chest in a surge of something very like relief.

"Drusilla and Rob are finally getting married," he murmured, more for his own edification than anything else. He might have known Coach would pick up on that.

"That's what I been saying for the past five minutes. Those two are getting hitched. Why else d'ya think they'd have a wedding shower?"

"Wasn't thinking, I guess." Tucker grinned as his glance sought and found Rob, his high school buddy— the only guy in their graduating class who'd never wanted more than the cattle and the spread his daddy had raised him on. Except for Drusilla. Rob had always wanted Dru.

"Well, they took long enough." Tucker chuckled at the lovesick pair. Some things never changed!

"You should talk!" Coach glared at him, and the warmth in his eyes frosted over. "What's this I hear about you getting engaged to some bird called Amanda DuPres?" His lips made a mockery of the old Bostonian name.

Did the whole world know?

"I'm not sure what you heard, Coach." Tucker's hands fisted at his sides, but he hung on to his composure out of sheer willpower. "Doesn't matter anyway, I suppose. Amanda is a wonderful woman and a good friend, but we're not getting married. I made a mistake."

"Of course it was a mistake, you idiot! You're not

the type for some fancy rich girl. Doesn't matter how far you go. The Junction's your home. That won't change.'' Coach whacked him on the back once more, for good measure, his mismatched teeth sparkling in a grin of pure happiness.

Tucker checked, but no one else had noticed them, not yet, anyway. He relaxed, gave in to the urge and let himself drown in the sight of her just once more.

Everything about Ginny was so—normal. Her big green eyes sparkled and shone as she teased Riley. Her lips still curved in that wholehearted grin, generous, nothing held back. Her hands still fluttered around when she spoke, accenting her words with a touch here, a motion there.

But it was Ginny's hair—that glossy, bouncing mane of almost black curls that refused to be constrained— that held his scrutiny the longest. Tucker almost laughed out loud. How many times had his high school Ginny despaired of her naturally curly hair? She'd tried the shorn-sheep look, the straight look, the scraped back and tied tight look. None of them worked. Ginny's curls simply would not obey. They rioted across her scalp however they wished, proclaiming her—what did that guy at the French station in Paris call it?

Joie de vivre—the joy of life.

That was Ginny, all right, bubbling joy. Tonight she looked very happy.

Tucker's eyes strayed to her hair. Once he'd loved the touch of those curls. Once—a lifetime ago.

One hand lifted of its own accord to rub the healing tissue on his face as Tucker soaked in the rest of her, clad tonight in a brilliant turquoise velour pantsuit that begged you to brush your fingers against the glossy threads.

She was so *alive*. That realization took some of the sting out of seeing her with Riley.

Tucker bent slightly, searched and eventually found what he was looking for. Now he knew he was home. Ginny's crazy shoes!

"Eye bothering you, son?"

Coach's murmured question brought home his actions. Tucker dropped the hand from his face like a brick. He straightened, grim reality washing away the memories. Ginny wasn't the same any more than he was.

"Tuck?"

"It doesn't hurt as much anymore. Scar tissue gets itchy sometimes, that's all."

He hated the sympathy he saw in the older man's face. Grief grabbed at him, made him wiggle with guilt. Tucker Townsend didn't deserve sympathy. Not when he'd gotten the injury and not now. Tucker was alive.

Quint wasn't.

"When did you get the eye patch off?" Coach led him to the buffet table, poured some punch, loaded a plate and then indicated two empty chairs in a corner of the room.

"Last week. I wear dark glasses during the day. The light still bothers me a little." Tucker lifted his glass, peered at the concoction in the punch bowl and wrinkled his nose when the pungent aroma of cranberries wafted up. "Did Mrs. Wheeler make the punch?"

"You should know by now that Ethel Wheeler always makes the punch. Life hasn't changed much in Jubilee Junction, son, no matter how you found the rest of the world. Leastways, the important stuff's stayed the same." Coach took a bite of his sandwich, chewed for a moment, then washed it down with the cranberry punch. He smirked.

"Well, maybe one thing's changed. I almost like this stuff now." One eyebrow flicked upward. "We've got the spare room ready, Tuck."

"No, that's not necessary. I'm already booked in at the motel." Tucker frowned, dismay filling him. "I'll be fine, Coach."

"No way." Coach shook his head decisively. "The wife's been looking forward to feeding you ever since you called yesterday. Cleaned the whole house just on your account. Singing like a hen with a chick come home. She won't hear tell of you bunking over there."

"But—"

"Forget it! Arguing with that woman isn't an option. Not when she's baking those goodies." Coach licked his lips, then winked, the love shining from his face like a beacon.

Love. What was it like to feel love like that?

"You staying in town long?"

It was the one question Tucker didn't want to answer. He didn't even know why he was here. His parents had long since moved to Minneapolis, divorced and found new lives. His siblings were spread across the country, involved in problems of their own. There was nothing in Jubilee Junction for him now.

And yet, he'd had to come, had to see if he could find any comfort here. Jubilee Junction was his last resort.

Ginny was his last hope.

"Tucker? Tucker, is that you?"

His heart picked up double time. His palms started to sweat. He gulped, then glanced up. Ginny.

"Yeah, it's me." He urged his legs to lift him up

and hold his aching body erect, forced himself to meet her stare. "How are you, Gin?"

"I'm fine, of course." Her green eyes swirled with worry as she inspected his battered face. Then her arms swept around his neck, and she hugged him tightly, burying her face in his chest. "Oh, I'm so glad you're all right, Tucker. We were worried when we heard you'd been hurt. Africa seems so far away from here, global village or not."

His arms came up of their own accord and curved around her waist, holding her close for as long as she wanted to be there. Her curls, soft as silk and just as shiny, tumbled over her shoulders, caressing his cheek as they danced across his shirt.

Tucker's nose caught her familiar scent—Persian roses. Spicy, soft, heady. She smelled like joy, and peace and comfort. She smelled like home.

"That means a lot to me, Ginny," he managed when she finally tugged away. "Thanks." He let her go, shuttered off the pain when she stepped back and Riley's proprietary arm flopped over her shoulders.

"Hi, Riley. How's the ranch?" Tucker winced as lean, muscular fingers tightened around his.

"About the same." Riley frowned, loosened his grip. "You okay, Tucker? You look like a north wind could flatten you."

Honesty was always the best policy.

"I feel like it, too." Tucker grinned, then sank back down into his chair before he fell down. "Seems like everything takes a little more effort than it used to, but I'll be fine. Healing is just a matter of time."

Ha! He'd just told the biggest lie of his life. Tucker would never be fine again. A man had died, and it was his fault. How did you heal from an injury as fatal as that?

He stared at his hands, wondering why he'd talked himself into coming here.

"I'm sorry about your friend, Tucker." Ginny's long slim fingers reached out and brushed across his cheek, shifting Riley's arm off her shoulders.

She'd homed in on his thoughts—again.

"It must be hard for you. If there's anything I can do…"

He nodded, unwilling to talk about it yet. She could do a lot, but he'd have to ease into that when Riley wasn't around.

"Thanks, Gin. But I'll be fine." His voice came out gruff, rejecting. Shame welled up inside when Ginny's face altered. He saw a flash of hurt wing through her eyes.

"Congratulations are in order for you, too. We heard about your engagement." Riley grinned, obviously thrilled. "When's the big day?"

"There's not going to be one." Tucker refused to say any more, to explain something that couldn't be explained.

He'd known as soon as he proposed that he couldn't marry Amanda. It just took a while to make her understand that his skewed-up life couldn't be fixed by marrying her.

More pain he'd caused. Someone else hurt because of him.

"Oh. Sorry." Riley frowned, his eyes glancing from Tucker to the woman at his side.

Tucker was grateful for Coach's hand on his arm, drawing his attention from a confused-looking Ginny. He wanted to explain, but what could he say? That he'd proposed to Amanda out of some last-ditch effort to make sense of his life? Not hardly.

Tucker nodded at the couple, rose to his feet and turned away, pretending to follow Coach's conversation. The truth was it was easier not to see Ginny sharing and laughing with Riley. Maybe if he didn't look, he wouldn't feel so alone.

Tucker made himself face the truth. This mood, this emptiness—it wasn't about Ginny, not really. It was about change. Seven years ago he'd made a promise, and he'd never kept it. Seven years ago he'd left her alone. She deserved whatever happiness she'd found.

Back then Ginny had read his thoughts as easily as he'd read hers. She always knew exactly when he was hurting, when to be there with a soft word, a prayer, a new insight.

This trip down memory lane was futile. Those days were long gone. He'd tossed them away as if they meant nothing.

Fool!

Oh, how he wanted to resurrect them.

Tucker kissed Mrs. Bains's cheek and let her tease him about not eating properly. By the time he turned back, Ginny and Riley were across the room, strolling away from him and his problems.

It was obvious her life was full and happy. She'd moved on. So why was he clinging to hope that a woman he'd promised to marry, then hadn't even spoken to in seven long years, would help him?

Somehow Ginny said all the right words, smiled, laughed, wished the blissful couple every happiness. Somehow she kept her back turned.

Somehow she kept her eyes off Tucker Townsend.

But inside, her heart cried out to God for answers.

Why didn't he look at her, really look at her, the way he had seven years ago? Why had God let Tucker Townsend come back if he was only going to ignore her?

"Are you about ready to leave?"

Riley's hand touched hers, but there was no ripple of excitement there. Not like Tucker's touch had once caused. Did that mean something, or was she just such a schoolgirl back then that everything Tucker had done seemed to spark excitement? Why did the past suddenly seem faded and worn?

"Yes, I'm ready. It's been a long day."

They left quietly through a side door, anxious not to disrupt those who stayed behind. The soft April air boasted just the slightest fragrance from newly budding flowers. Overhead the stars glimmered against a blue velvet sky.

Spring. A time of new beginnings.

Tucker was back.

"It's a beautiful night. I'll walk you to your car." Riley threaded her arm through his when Ginny wobbled on her high heels. "I could have picked you up, you know. You didn't have to drive over."

Something funny in his voice snagged her attention. He'd sounded almost—proprietorial. Ginny frowned.

"Riley, I always drive myself. You know that. Besides, I was on a consultation till six-thirty."

"And you're probably too tired to walk anywhere now, aren't you?"

Her throbbing feet were caused by heels far too high to be worn for an entire day. But Ginny wasn't going to admit that. Not yet. Besides, something told her Riley needed to talk. In the past few months, as they'd become better friends, she'd grown adept at hearing the signals in his voice that meant he finally wanted to speak of whatever was brewing behind his dark, thoughtful gaze.

Ginny hugged her white angora cape closer. The night breeze kicked up a notch, penetrating her suit just enough to raise the hairs on her skin. She hoped Riley would hurry and say whatever was bothering him. She wanted to get away and think about tonight, about Tucker.

How stupid was that?

The town's newly developed park lay just across the street. It was here Riley led her, down a path where big spruce boughs offered protection from the wind and seclusion from the prying eyes that always watched in Jubilee Junction.

Ginny stared in pleased surprise when Riley eventually stopped beside a hearth of stones. In seconds he had a small fire crackling merrily in the little pit. A bench sat nearby, out of the smoke but still close enough to feel the heat of the coals. Ginny sank onto it with relief.

"You had this all arranged." She marveled at his quick thinking. "I walked here on my lunch hour, and this hearth wasn't here."

He smiled.

"I slipped out earlier, while you were serving coffee. I thought maybe we could talk for a minute." Riley folded his lean body next to hers on the wrought-iron bench.

"Of course we can talk. It was sweet of you to think of a fire. I haven't been near a campfire since I took my church class camping last summer. And you know what a disaster that was!" She giggled at the memory.

"I guess I'd forgotten how important it is for a teenager to be cool."

Cool, she remembered, had never mattered to Tucker. Seven years ago he hadn't cared that her hair never obeyed, that she'd lost the canoe race for his team. He'd laughed and celebrated with her anyway. They'd been each other's cheering section then, a mutual support pair.

She got lost in the memories.

"Ginny?"

"Yes?" The note of urgency in Riley's voice snagged her attention. Ginny berated her selfishness. Always Tucker. When would she grow up? "I'm sorry, Riley. Go ahead. I'm listening."

"Will you please do me the honor of becoming Mrs. Riley Cantrel?"

Ginny stared at him, utter shock dropping her jaw to her chest. Riley knelt before her, his hat on the ground. His fingers closed around hers.

"Uh, Riley, I—" She felt his fingers tighten.

"Just say yes. We'd have a good life on the ranch, Ginny. There's lots of room for kids to run and play, plenty of animals for pets. The house is just waiting for your special touch."

"But—but—" she sputtered, searching desperately for the right words and finding none. Where had this come from? Why hadn't she seen what he'd obviously been leading up to?

"I know I'm no Prince Charming. I live on a ranch with horses. I don't know all the fancy phrases women like to hear. I haven't traveled a lot or seen a whole bunch of places."

Like Tucker—was that what he meant? An idea glimmered at the back of Ginny's mind, but she didn't have time to pursue it. She lifted a hand, touched his cheek.

"When you're talking about marriage, I don't think traveling is as important as a lot of other things, Riley," she whispered, studying his handsome face. "I think love is more important."

"I can learn to love you, Ginny. It's just a matter of time. I know you've got your father's health and your own business to consider. I wouldn't dream of interfering in that. You're becoming very successful, and I'm glad for you."

Her father. Ginny could see his face, imagine the satisfaction he'd show at the news of her engagement. It wasn't fair that a man who loved children as much as her dad did had only been given one. Grandchildren would put the glint in Dad's eyes, something his recurring health problems had dimmed almost to nonexistence.

But it isn't good enough! It isn't the right reason to marry Riley. The plan was for you and Tucker to be together.

But was that still God's plan?

Lately God's will for her life hadn't been exactly clear to Ginny. She'd waited so long for answers—answers to her father's dwindling health, answers that would provide an opportunity to take the last two courses and finish her interior design degree, answers that would explain Tucker's long absence.

Of course, Dad's health was the most pressing. She could wait a little longer for Tucker and her degree, but her father needed a diagnosis. She'd watched and tried to carry the load, but still he slipped steadily downhill.

Why didn't God answer her anymore?

"So will you...marry me?"

Ginny drew her mind to the present, to Riley. She *did* care for him, but as a friend. Nothing more. Where had this sudden romantic impulse come from? And what could she say that wouldn't hurt him or embarrass him?

Ginny swallowed, praying for help as she tried to frame a response.

"I'm very honored you would choose me, Riley," she murmured at last, squeezing his hand. "But this is so sudden. I've always thought of us as friends. I never thought—that is, I never dreamed—" She sucked in a breath. "I hope that you'll understand when I say I have to think about it."

"As long as you don't say no, I'll be happy." He drew her up to stand beside him. His mouth brushed across her cheek in a gentle brotherly caress. "We could have a good future, Ginny. I'll always stick by you, no matter what. You can count on me."

Stick by her? What did he mean, no matter what?

"It's kind of a bad time for me just now, Riley," she murmured, trying to prepare him. "There's Dad and the store to think about. Dad's not getting any better. And then there's Tucker."

"Yeah. Tucker." Riley's eyes narrowed, darkened. "I don't think he'll be hanging around for long, Ginny. He's just back to show us all what a hotshot he's become."

"You may be right, though I'm not so sure. But even if he is, we had a promise, Riley," she reminded him softly. "I owe my first allegiance to Tucker."

"You don't owe Tucker Townsend anything!"

She'd never seen Riley so angry.

"It's been seven years, Ginny. Seven whole years! Has he written, even once? Did he phone or send a card on your birthday? At Christmas? Did he even know you were still here?"

"No, but—"

"And you think he's going to abide by some silly teenage promise?" Riley's voice softened. His hand rose to cup her cheek. "He won't, Ginny. I'm sorry, but as soon as Tucker Townsend heals up, he'll be off into the wild blue yonder building his image, and you'll be left waiting. You don't want that."

She couldn't say anything. Not now. However Riley had come by his decision to propose, she owed him the dignity of a well-thought-out response, not a rush of words defending Tucker.

"We could be happy, Ginny. I know we could. And neither of us would be alone."

The clock tower bonged ten strokes, snapping the spell that held her transfixed. She had to think this through. Better to take her time. Ginny eased herself out of his grip.

"I promise you I will think about it, Riley. And I'll let you know my decision as soon as I can. All right?"

It was a long time before he answered. When he finally spoke, the fervor had died out of his eyes, leaving them bleak.

"Yeah. Sure." He bent to extinguish the fire without expression. "I knew it was a long shot, anyway."

No longer simply cool, the chilly breeze swept in tiny gusts, swirling around them just enough to remind them that winter wasn't far gone. It penetrated the wool of her cape to chill her skin all over again. Ginny shivered.

"I should have brought a blanket. Come on. Let's go."

Assured the fire was completely out, Riley wrapped an arm around her shoulders and hugged her against the warmth of his body as they trudged quickly toward the church.

Riley waited by her car until she'd unlocked it.

"Thank you for thinking of the fire, Riley, and for the romantic proposal. I'm honored you would ask me to be your wife. I promise I'll have an answer for you soon." Ginny tilted forward on her spiky heels and pressed a quick kiss against his skin. She would have climbed into her car then, but his hand on her arm prevented that.

Ginny glanced up. Her whole body froze as she followed Riley's gaze across the street to the big man limping down the lane beside the older, shriveled figure of their former coach.

One finger under her chin forced her eyes to meet his.

"Is it because of him?" Riley's low voice sounded grave. "Have you still got feelings for the guy, Ginny, or is it duty to the past that makes Tucker the reason you can't say yes to me?"

She'd hurt him, and that was the last thing Ginny wanted to do. She laid her hand on Riley's arm, begged him to hear what she wasn't saying.

"Riley, you've been my friend for a very long time, and I care about you. It's true that I believed it was God's will for Tucker and me to be together. As silly as that sounds, I guess I still believe that." She took a deep breath. "But I don't know what's happened to him. I don't know why he's back. So, yes, in a way I guess Tucker is part of the reason I'm asking for time."

"You didn't say if you were still in love with him."

"No, I didn't."

He frowned at her non-response.

Ginny smiled. One thing she could count on with

Riley was his persistence—he didn't give up his plans easily.

"I've got to pray about your proposal, Riley, seek the Lord's will. Then I'll give you my answer."

Without saying a word, they both turned to watch Tucker and Coach enter the small bungalow at the end of the street. Minutes passed. Finally Riley spoke.

"I'm a careful man, Ginny," he murmured, his fingers tensing on her shoulders. "I don't like mistakes. I'll be praying about this, too. I want someone to share Christmas and New Year's eve with, someone who cares about me. Someone who isn't pining after a dream."

Riley was a rancher. He seldom spoke at all, let alone sweet nothings. This quiet speech touched Ginny deeply.

"I know you're lonely, Riley. I am, too, sometimes." She touched his cheek with her fingers. "But marriage needs more than that to be successful."

"Yeah." He sighed, then dredged up a smile. "Take all the time you need, Ginny. I'll be out of town for a while, anyway."

Riley bent, pressed a light, hurried kiss on her cheek, then stalked to his truck, parked behind the church. He never looked back.

Ginny stood there watching him until her feet reminded her they wanted to be free. She climbed in her car, kicked off her shoes and turned on the heat. Then she flipped open her cell phone.

"Hi, Dad. Everything okay?"

Assured that her father was drowsing through the news and didn't need her home immediately, Ginny put her car into gear and drove, not even realizing until she parked that she'd driven straight to Pinetree Bluff—Tucker's favorite spot.

As she sat in her car on the promontory overlooking the town, Ginny finally loosed her thoughts, let all the worries, doubts and fears pour out in a mishmash of questions.

Riley Cantrel wanted to marry her. He was a good man, solid, reliable. He wasn't flashy, didn't throw money around, seldom said anything he didn't mean. He believed in the same things she did, went to the same church, shared her faith in God. He would make a good husband.

For someone else.

She sighed, the truth worming its way to her brain. Why pretend?

Then she remembered Riley's question. Was she still in love with Tucker? The answer haunted her because she didn't know who Tucker Townsend was anymore. What had he become?

Seven years ago Tucker had promised to marry Ginny. She'd waited, prayed and kept herself busy while God worked out the details. But Tucker had never returned. Now all the logical reasoning in the world wouldn't quiet the voice muttering in the back of Ginny's head.

Was Tucker back to keep his promise to marry her? Or was he here for something else entirely, something that would only take him away again?

He hadn't acted as if he'd come back for her, hadn't even spent much time talking to her tonight. Certainly he hadn't suggested another meeting. So what did it mean? She'd kept the faith, done her part, believed, hoped, trusted. Why didn't God make the answer clear?

Though the windshield, Ginny watched the northern

lights twist their yellow-purple bands in a slow-motion dance that needed no accompaniment. A new untried pattern rippled across the black silk sky, changing colors as it hung suspended in the night. Pure, unadulterated, simple yet glorious.

Free.

Ginny squeezed her eyes closed, took a deep breath and faced reality.

"Okay, God. Truth time. I like Riley, I like him a lot, but I don't want to marry him. I want what I've always wanted—to be Tucker's wife. I thought that's what You wanted, too. Was I wrong? Is there truth in Riley's words? Have I wasted seven years believing in something that isn't going to happen?"

The thought of it scared her, and she opened her eyes, waiting for some hint of reassurance. But in the stillness of the spring night the heavens kept silent. No response floated out to quiet the plethora of questions that raged inside her.

Ginny sighed. She'd have to tell Riley no. He was a good man, a friend, but she couldn't marry him. Not even if Tucker weren't in the picture. Truthfully, she hadn't even entertained the idea, not after the first shock. But how to tell him, what words to use? Perhaps if she went over it again, organized everything into pros and cons she could made some sense of order out of this mess.

"We're friends, just friends. He's wonderful, kind, gentle, but I don't love him. Really, I don't think he loves me, either." She tried to remember what had bothered her earlier about his proposal, but the thought would not return.

"Riley says he wants to marry me. He'd be a good husband, a handsome one."

The words from Sunday's sermon slipped back into her brain with sharp clarity.

We occupy ourselves with good things, well-meaning things, beneficial things. But are they the best things? Are they God's choice for us, or simply the result of our own scheming to get what we believe we must have?

"I know—I can't marry Riley. But I don't understand, God. What are You trying to tell me? What is Your plan for me if it isn't Tucker?"

The green glow of the numbers on the dashboard caught her glance as the hour turned over. A new day would soon begin.

"The first day of the rest of my life," she whispered. "But what will that life be like? Will I go on, hoping and waiting, never seeing an answer to my prayers?"

The reality of it staggered her. Seven years gone, disappeared since graduation night when she'd looked out on the world and made her plans. Sure, some things hadn't happened the way she'd wanted. But she'd taken what God had sent and done the best she could with it. She'd made a life for herself, built new plans when the old ones hadn't worked. She'd followed God's leading as closely as she knew.

So why, tonight of all nights, did Tucker's promise seem so impossible?

You'll be my bride, Ginny. I promise.

A tear trickled down her face.

"Will it finally happen, God? I want the love and commitment other women have. I want my own family, a future with a man I can share it with. Jubilee Junction's my home, I can't leave Dad. What about Tucker? Why don't I feel Your reassurance that things will be all right now?"

A thought swam into her mind and grew more logical every second she thought about it.

"It's nerves." She said it out loud, the words sending a rush of relief through her veins. "Just a silly case of awkward jitters. Tucker's been away a long time. He'll need a few days to get things back into perspective, especially since his best friend is dead. I just have to be patient a little longer."

In seven years, patience had solved a lot of problems for Ginny. Maybe it would again.

"All right, then," she told herself, studying the glow of the streetlights of Jubilee Junction in the shallow valley below her. "I'll just wait for Tucker to come to me. Once he's settled in, we'll pick up where we left off. Then we'll talk about marriage. I'm sure of it."

She hunched over the wheel to catch the sky's changing patterns. A pink hue banded a wide swath from east to west. Wasn't that a heavenly blessing on her decision?

Ginny nodded. "Patience, girl. Let him make the first move."

An unopened can of soda sat in the cup holder. She flipped the top open and held up the tin in a toast to herself.

"Well, Virginia Brown, your dreams may finally be coming true. Go boldly forward. Don't ever look back."

She took a swig of the drink, then wiggled her nose as the sickly sweet liquid rolled down her throat and bubbles tickled inside her nose. The vent blew directly on the can and had heated the soda to a lukewarm fizzle that didn't appeal. Ginny decided to dump the rest.

Perhaps that was why she didn't notice until it was too late to protest.

The passenger door opened, and Tucker Townsend

climbed inside, eyes glinting with a remnant of that old boyish charm.

"Hi, Gin. I knew I'd find you here."

He knew? He remembered this spot, but he didn't remember his promise?

"Hi, Tucker." She emptied the soda onto the ground outside her window, then thrust the empty can into the bag she kept for just such a purpose. "I didn't expect to see you out here so late." Let him make the first move.

"It's not that late, Gin. You don't still have a curfew, do you?" His smile slashed across his scarred face and begged her to play along.

"A self-imposed one," she told him. She wiggled her toes in the wave of warm air she had directed downward. "I should be getting home. I'm sure you're tired, too. Couldn't we talk tomorrow, Tucker?"

"Sure." He picked up her shoes, whistled, then tossed them into the back seat. "Some things never change. You're still trying to make a statement, aren't you, Gin?"

He sounded—disinterested. As if he didn't really care. Ginny frowned.

"I don't have to make a statement here," she told him. "Everyone knows me, knows who I am, what I am. I've lived in Jubilee Junction a long time, Tucker. I'm the same person I always was. What you see is exactly what you get."

His eyes stayed on her, assessing, studying, considering.

"I know," he murmured. "That's what I counted on."

"What you counted on?" A hot tide of embarrassment rose up her neck. That didn't sound like a compliment. It sure didn't sound like a man who could hardly wait to reunite with the woman he'd promised to marry!

Ginny shifted the car into gear, biting her trembling lip. This wasn't what she'd planned at all. Now that Tucker was finally home, all she wanted was to run away from that cool, calculating look in his eyes.

"We can talk tomorrow, Tucker."

"Wait!" His hand came out, stopped hers. "Please, just wait a minute."

Reluctantly, Ginny returned the gearshift to Park. She leaned back in her seat, tugged her hand from beneath his and waited. When he didn't speak, she finally glanced up.

His face had lost all animation, and what little color he'd had earlier had drained away. Her heart picked up its beat at the cheekbones jutting out, but she ruthlessly ignored the urge to soothe. Something told her now was the time for hard truth.

"What do you want from me, Tucker?"

"Help." His voice burst out on a ragged plea that echoed through her car.

"Help?" She stared at him. That was it? Confusion rippled through her brain. "Help with what?"

This didn't make any sense. Tucker's fingers clenched the armrest, his body ramrod stiff in his seat, his eyes glazed over with something that made Ginny cringe in fear.

"Help with facing the truth." The words seemed to choke out of their own volition, as if he resisted saying them but couldn't stop them.

"What truth?"

His breath whooshed out in short gasps. He looked

at her, and the wealth of suffering in his eyes brought tears to hers.

"Tucker, please. Tell me what's wrong. I'm trying to understand, but you have to tell me."

"Thanks, Gin, but I see now that it was a mistake to come here. You can't help." He lifted a hand, touched her cheek with a dry, mirthless smile, then let it fall away. "No one can. The blame sits squarely on me, and I can't avoid it, no matter how hard I try."

"What blame?" She was afraid to hear him say it, whatever it was. Something dark, menacing, clung to him. Something she sensed could cause havoc with her cherished plans.

"I've done a terrible thing, Gin. I've committed a crime worse than the ones I've spent seven years covering. I'm no better than a murderer. That's why God's abandoned me."

Chapter Two

"Tucker!"

Ginny couldn't help the gasp that burst from her. Nor could she stop staring at him, trying to figure out what had changed about Tucker Townsend that made him seem both harsh and yet so pitiful.

"Wh-what do you mean—murderer?" She whispered the words with a trickle of dread she couldn't quite conceal. "Tucker, that's ridiculous! Don't say it again."

"Why not? It's true."

She watched the despair cloud his eyes, the discouragement hunch his shoulders. This broken man showed none of the brash, take-it-on-the-chin characteristics the old Tucker had reveled in.

Ginny tried again, strove to find something to cheer him. Encouragement, that always worked.

"Tucker, God doesn't abandon anyone."

"Doesn't He?" His brown eyes flickered, stared into hers, then he peered out the windshield. His grim countenance didn't alter one whit. "He's abandoned me."

"You don't really believe that. Do you?" Ginny frowned, uncertainty dogging her.

"Yes."

How could she argue with such obvious hopelessness?

"Well, you're wrong. God is always there, always listening, always hearing, waiting for us to return to Him."

Brave words. Her conscience applauded. But for all their sanctimonious sound, they didn't dent Tucker's torture. He shook his head wearily.

"Only for so long. Then He gives up. I stepped over that threshold, Ginny. I should have realized I was going too far, that I was asking too much, but I willfully kept pushing until a man died. Because of me."

There it was again, that implication that he'd committed some crime. Why? What was behind this?

Ginny was about to speak when the shrill peal of her phone echoed around the inside of her car. The sound stopped the words on her lips. What now?

"Dad?" He was the only one who would be calling her at this time of night. "Are you all right, Dad?"

A yawning silence, then the agonized words.

"I need help, honey."

That was all she needed to hear.

"I'll be there in less than five minutes. Hang on, Dad. Hang on." She clicked the phone shut, shifted the car into gear and began backing out, only to realize that Tucker was still seated beside her.

"I have to go. You'd better get out now, go back in your own vehicle."

"I walked. I'll go with you. Maybe there's something I can do to help." A ripple of interest brought amazing life into his battered face.

Ginny didn't argue. She couldn't, she had to get home. As she drove down the hill and wheeled around curves in a shortcut to her home, she bit her lip.

She should have been at home, should have been right there for her father, instead of mooning over a man who only wanted her *help*.

So Tucker was back—what did that mean to her? Of course she was sorry he'd been injured, that he had questions about his faith. But didn't everyone? What made him think she had any answers?

With a jerk, Ginny braked to a halt in her driveway, her eyes riveted on the old brick house.

"Please God, let him be all right."

She searched for her shoes, remembered Tucker had tossed them in the back seat and abandoned the quest. She grabbed her keys from the console, shoved her door open and raced to the front door, ignoring the cold that stabbed against the soles of her feet through her thin stockings. What did a little cold matter when her father was sick?

Her fingers fumbled as she fought to unlock the door.

"I'll do it." Tucker took her keys, clicked the lock, then thrust open the door without hesitation. "Go."

Ginny flew into the den after one startled moment. Tucker was still here?

Her father lay hunched over in his recliner, hands clenching his side, his face pinched and gray with pain.

"When did you take the last pill?" Ginny demanded, checking for signs of distress in the shriveled figure. "Dad?" Her fingers circled his wrist, counting off the beats as she'd been taught.

"Didn't take it," he gasped, his eyes flickering open long enough to take in the sight of his daughter and the man behind her. "Thought I could manage without." He closed his eyes, wincing with pain. "Stupid."

"Very." Forcing herself to calm down, Ginny strode to the bathroom, grabbed the kit the doctor had given her for just such emergencies and selected what she needed. Then she hurried back to the den.

Tucker stood beside her father, his eyes almost black in the light from the lamp. When he saw what she carried, he rolled up her father's sleeve without being asked.

"Thanks."

Ginny uncapped the syringe. In sure, steady moves that hid her stammering nerves, she swiped the area with an alcohol swab, then plunged the needle directly into her father's muscle and emptied the liquid into his system.

It took less than two minutes for the drug to take effect. Gradually the grayness eased, the fingers unclenched, the weary body relaxed.

"Thanks, honey. I fell asleep here, didn't realize I'd left my pills upstairs. Then the pain started and I couldn't get to them. It was pretty bad this time." He apologized bashfully, his face regaining its smile as he spoke.

"You're supposed to keep them with you at all times." She knew her voice was sharp, but Ginny couldn't help it. He'd scared her. "You can't afford to forget, Dad. You've got to keep yourself healthy. Staying up late, drinking this—" she picked up the half cup of coffee and raised an eyebrow "—none of it helps. You know what the doctors said. Until they figure out what's causing this…"

"I know. Don't fuss. It was just one cup, honey. It's been so long since I had a decent cup of coffee."

"Nobody in their right mind would call this coffee decent," she muttered, plopping the tarry concoction down.

Ginny saw him sigh and relented, knowing just how hard it was for her father to do without all the things he loved. Taken in the whole, coffee was a relatively small transgression.

"Time for bed, Dad. Can you make it up the stairs?" She ignored Tucker's gasp of surprise as her sickly father faltered to his feet, his thin arms shaking with the effort of elevating himself.

"I'll be fine." Adrian Brown ignored his daughter, his focus entirely on Tucker.

"Hello, sir. It's good to see you again."

"You're back." The words were noncommital.

"Yes."

"For how long?"

"I'm not sure." To his credit, Tucker didn't back down, even though the frosty tone should have quelled him. He glanced at Ginny. "I guess that depends on your daughter."

Ginny's head whirled around so fast she saw stars.

"On me?" she squeaked, joy fluttering with apprehension at his words. "What does your visit here have to do with me?"

Adrian Brown nodded. "Good question. I'd like to know the answer myself."

It was obvious Tucker was uncomfortable. His lids drooped over his eyes, hiding whatever explanation Ginny might have found there. His hands knotted in front of him. Then, as he became aware of what he was doing, he tore them apart and shoved them into his pockets.

"I take it you didn't return to keep your promise."

Ginny almost laughed as her father's cranky tones broke the yawning silence with the one question that lay uppermost on her mind. Dad must be feeling better. Trust him to blurt out what everyone else was thinking.

She glanced at Tucker.

Devastation slapped her in the face as he shifted his glance away from hers, his face tinged the faint pink of embarrassment. Truth plunged through her heart. He wasn't back to marry her. He probably hadn't even given the promise a second thought.

Ginny scrambled to hide her hurt.

"It doesn't matter why he's back, Dad. His problems can wait." She wanted her father tucked up in bed. Now.

Ginny's father snorted his disgust. "I'm not dying, you know. It was just a little spell. It didn't render me brainless. Tell me why you're here, Tucker."

"I can't. I have to talk it over with Ginny first."

Ginny didn't dare think what his words meant. Tucker thrust his chin out belligerently as he glared at the older man. She was fairly certain Tucker hadn't been ordered around for years. Clearly he didn't like it. But her father wasn't backing down, either.

"My daughter and I have no secrets from each other. I'm sure she won't mind if you let me in on this little conundrum of yours." Little by little Adrian regained some of his height.

Ginny frowned. The last part of her father's sentence came out whisper soft. His fingers tightened around her arm as he struggled to remain upright. He wasn't all right. He needed rest, not more problems. Why couldn't Tucker have waited, saved whatever he had to say until she got her father to bed?

Why didn't he ask his former fiancée for help?

The one he proposed to when he was supposed to marry *her?*

It was an uncharitable thought and one she immediately regretted. But the weight of all her problems seemed too heavy tonight. She felt stretched out, overextended.

"Sorry, boys," she interjected, her voice sharp. "We're not doing this right now. Come on, Dad. You need to go to bed. It doesn't matter what Tucker wants to ask me. Whatever it is, it can wait."

She saw Tucker's mouth open in protest and flashed him a look that silenced him.

"We'll visit with Tucker tomorrow, Dad. You can talk all you want. But for now, I think you need to rest."

Her father nodded, turned to cross the room in his halting gait.

"Maybe you're right, honey. I do feel kind of shaky." He patted the hand still threaded through his arm. "Thanks for getting here so fast, Ginny."

She bussed his cheek with her fist.

"And no speeding ticket, either," she teased.

She helped her father up the stairs, waited while he undressed, then tucked him in bed, ensuring his pills were in plain view on the nightstand, right beside his water.

"That shot should take care of things for tonight. If you feel like you need a pill, you'd better call me first. I want to read the doctor's instructions. There's supposed to be a lapse of time after the shot."

"I won't need another pill. I'm too tired to stay awake." Her father's pallid face faded into the white of his pillowcase. "I'll be fine in the morning."

"Of course you will. Good night, Dad. Sleep well."

She leaned down to kiss his cheek, her eyes alert for any signs of pain or discomfort. She found none.

"Ginny?" His hand reached up to grasp hers. "Whatever Tucker wants, regardless of your past, you know you'll have to help him, don't you?"

She frowned. "Why do you say that?"

"That boy's in trouble, honey. You can see it in his eyes." His forehead pleated in a frown. "I don't know why he hightailed it back to this neck of the woods, but it's obvious he's looking for something. After seven years, it must be something mighty big to send him back here."

"He's got a lot of questions about God, Dad. I think he just needs some faith bolstering." Ginny shrugged as if it didn't matter one way or the other that Tucker hadn't mentioned marriage. "I'll send him on to the pastor. He's a good counselor."

"He is, but I don't think Tucker can find what he needs from the pastor. I think he's depending on you." Adrian's eyes flopped closed, and his breathing slowed to a regular rhythm that told her his medication had finally taken over.

"Good night, Dad," she whispered, then tiptoed out of the room, pulling the door closed behind her.

By the time she made it to the bottom of the stairs, Ginny drooped with fatigue. She wanted a cup of hot chocolate, a hot bath and lots of sleep. In that order. She certainly didn't want to deal with any more questions—her own or anyone else's.

"Is he all right?" Tucker stepped out of the shadows, his eyes dark, confused.

"For now." She walked past him into the kitchen. Tucker followed. Ginny ignored him and plugged the kettle in. "At least he'll sleep."

"He doesn't look well, Gin."

For some reason, the old nickname irritated her. She whirled to glare at him. Was that all he could think of to say to her—after seven years?

"That's because he isn't well," she blurted. She snatched two mugs out of the cupboard and spooned in hot-chocolate mix with careless abandon.

"What's wrong with him? Is it his heart or something? He never seemed like the kind of person who would have a heart attack. He's always so controlled." Tucker snagged a chair with his foot and sank into it.

"Things change, Tucker. So do people. Especially after seven years." With nothing else to do, Ginny sat down at the table opposite him.

"Yeah, I guess. I'm sorry."

Ginny refused to respond to that. He was sorry, but he didn't even know what he was sorry for! He simply waltzed back into town and expected everyone to be there.

"The doctors don't know exactly what the problem is, but they've ruled out heart. He's been through a whole pile of tests, but they still haven't figured it out."

The words burst out of her, bald, hard. The fear she felt came through as anger. Ginny glared at Tucker, willing him to see how hard this was.

"He gets pains. In different places. They can't seem to figure out why, to pinpoint the cause. And every day he gets a little weaker, the pain bites a little deeper. My father is a sick man."

"I had no idea." Tucker's mouth hung open in shock. He gulped but never looked away from her penetrating gaze. "I'm sorry, Virginia. I really didn't know."

The soft sincerity in those words was her undoing.

Ginny choked on a little sob and let the words that begged saying burst over him.

"Of course you didn't know. I wanted to tell you, to talk to you about it, but how could I? You disappeared from our lives and never bothered to check back." She hated doing this, but the worry had become too much. And still she had no answers.

"You stroll into town expecting everything in little old Jubilee Junction to be the same. You assumed we'd all be here, waiting to welcome you." She swallowed the tears and dared to say the words she'd hidden for so long.

"Did you ever think about us at all, Tucker? You never knew when some friend died or another moved away, when a couple split up and tore apart their family." She softened her voice, tried to make him understand. "Did you ever give a thought to how it was for the people who chose to stay in this town, to make it their home, to push through all the problems and find joy and peace and satisfaction in their ordinary lives?"

"No, I guess I didn't," he admitted softly.

She stared at him, seeing the old Tucker transposed onto this newer, harsher Tucker.

"Why not? You spent the first eighteen years of your life here. You grew up with me, lived next door, went to the same church. We shared precious childhood times together, and then you walked away from all of it, from me, as if I never existed."

"I went to college." He said it as if it explained everything.

It didn't. Ginny despised herself for harking back like this, but she had to say it. She'd been silent for too long.

"I know you did. Then you got a job, and another

one, and another, until finally you were top of the heap. You traveled all over the world, covered every major news story you could get near. You built a reputation for homing in on the heart of those horrible conflicts, of showing the human side of the suffering. I know exactly what you've been doing.''

The kettle whistled. Ginny rose, poured boiling water over the chocolate, then carried the mugs to the table.

''You kept track of me?'' He sounded shocked.

''Of course we did.'' She smiled, sadness creeping over her. ''You were one of us, the one who went out into the big bad world and accomplished something worthwhile. You were our ambassador and we were proud.''

''I—I didn't know.''

She stirred her drink so vigorously the brown liquid overflowed the cup and ran in a little river across the polished surface. Did he even care? She mopped the mess, heart aching.

''Of course you didn't know. How could you? You never came back, never wrote, never phoned. We never mattered enough to you—your history meant nothing to you.'' She shrugged. Her voice dropped to a whisper. ''Apparently I didn't mean anything, either.''

He shook his head, eyes downcast. ''That isn't the way it was, Gin.''

''Really?'' She looked through her lashes, dared him to refute what she'd come to believe was the truth. ''Weren't you just a little bit ashamed of us, Tucker? Wasn't it embarrassing to admit that your roots were among common, ordinary people who wouldn't even know where Sri Lanka is, let alone what's happening there?''

''I have never, ever been ashamed of Jubilee Junction

or its inhabitants.'' His angry glare gave testament to his words. ''Never.''

''Fine.'' She shrugged, tired of the whole thing. ''It doesn't really matter. It's the past. Maybe I should leave it there.''

''Ginny, if this is about that promise I made you—''

''It's not.'' She cut him off, hid her pain behind bravado. ''That promise meant nothing. Did you think I don't know that? Haven't figured it out after seven years?''

The bitterness, the gall of it ate into her heart like acid. How stupid she'd been.

''Of course it meant something.'' Tucker's face blushed a rich, dark red as he met her skeptical glance. ''I meant what I said. I was going to marry you.''

''Really?'' She shook her head, wishing he'd deny it. ''I don't think so, Tucker. It was just something kids say before they leave the nest. It was your way of hanging on to something secure when you stepped into the unknown. I should have figured that out after you left. When you didn't come back.''

''How could you figure it out when I fully intended to come back? I *did* intend to marry you.''

''When, Tucker?'' She played with the mug, which no longer held any interest. Ginny waited, hoping he'd stop her, tell her she was wrong, tell her he still loved her.

He didn't say anything.

''When were we to be married, Tucker? When you didn't write even one letter from college? When you didn't let us know you'd won that prestigious scholarship? When you didn't visit even once in seven years? When were you going to find time for marriage? For me?''

"I know, Gin. I should have written." He raked a hand through his hair, his eyes swirling with emotion. "But at first I had to work a lot to supplement the scholarship. My dad sure wouldn't chip in." His bottom lip curled with disgust.

She frowned. His father hadn't wanted Tucker to go away.

"Then I got caught up in the work, in the excitement." His hands fluttered through the air as he tried to explain. "When you're covering a story, time loses all relevance. I spent six months buried in the Amazon and never even knew I'd been gone a week."

"I understand," she lied. She didn't understand. Surely if you loved someone—but that was the point. He didn't love her. Ginny gulped and told the truth as she understood it.

"I believe everything and everyone came second once you were on a story. The job meant everything." She stared at him, trying to figure out exactly who Tucker Townsend had become.

"You know, Tucker, at first I wanted to leave, to be with you. I wanted to take my design degree, just as we'd planned."

"But you didn't."

Ginny almost smiled. The challenge in those words stung—as if she'd been the one to forget their promise!

"My mother passed away. Dad couldn't manage things alone. I had to stay, to help."

"I—I'm sorry."

"I'm not." She shook her head, letting her hair loose in hopes of easing the strain on her neck. "I grew to like working in the store, matching fabrics and designs to people's personalities and homes. I took courses by correspondence, even managed to attend some short college sessions on campus."

She smiled, remembering some of her less than remarkable projects.

"I tried out everything I learned in the houses around town and got more experience than I ever would have found in school, no matter how hard I studied. Eventually I developed a side business of my own."

"So you're happy here?" He sounded as if he didn't quite believe what she was saying.

"I'm very happy." Ginny shrugged. "There have been some hard times. Dad's been sick, but he's hanging on."

"His medical bills must be high."

"Astronomical." Ginny grimaced. "But we manage. I'm doing a lot of custom work now."

"I suppose that's why you've been seeing Riley—to get financial help? Riley always was good at figures."

She didn't like the question, didn't like the implication behind it. Ginny stared him down, relieved when Tucker finally looked away.

"Riley is a very good friend," she murmured. "He's been here whenever we needed him."

"Point taken. Sorry." He didn't look sorry. He looked fractious, ready for a fight. Then his eyes rested on her face, softened, filled with sympathy. "I really am sorry, Gin. I had no right to bother you, especially not tonight. You must be so concerned."

"Apology accepted." Ginny smiled to show no hard feelings, but kept her emotions firmly under control. She was tired. She was worn-out. If she ranted and raged as she wanted, she would say things she'd regret. It was better to pretend life was a bowl of cherries.

"Which brings us back to my father's question. Why

does your stay in Jubilee Junction depend on me?'' She sat quietly, hands folded in her lap as she waited.

When he didn't reply, Ginny frowned, lifting her eyes to study his face.

Tucker Townsend lost for words?

"I'll listen, Tucker," she whispered, covering his hand on the table with hers. "Whatever you have to say, I will listen."

He threaded his fingers through hers, his eyes steady on her face. Something fluttered through his brown gaze, but it was gone as quickly as it came. He raked a hand through his dark hair, huffed in a great quantity of air, then exhaled it in one whoosh.

"I counted on that," he admitted quietly. "I came back because I need you to help me, Gin." His words rebounded around the kitchen, a desperate plea, even though his voice had dropped to a deadly, whisper-soft calm.

Ginny stared. "Help you do what?"

"Help me figure out what's wrong. I need a way to get God to listen to me, to hear me, to tell me how I can go back to a job I think I hate. I need you to explain how I can find God when He's turned His back on me." The words poured out in desperation.

Ginny gulped, shocked by the admittance, stunned by the truth she saw reflected in his eyes. They were wide open, laid bare for her inspection. His shame, private agony and fear touched her in a place Ginny thought long dead. It hurt to witness his pain.

"But, Tuck." She fell back on the old nickname without thinking. "I'm not a minister or a priest. I can't counsel or advise you in something like this. This is a matter between you and your spiritual leader."

"I don't have one." His voice tightened to a harsh

grate. "I've attended a lot of churches lately, looked for answers. There's nothing there. God doesn't hear and He doesn't answer. Not me, anyway." He paused. Swallowed. "I even saw a psychiatrist."

"And?"

The twist of his lips proclaimed his anguish.

"That's not the kind of help I need." His eyes were riveted on her. "I need someone who can help me break the silence."

Ginny heard the implication through a mist of unbelief. Her? Surely Tucker couldn't be serious?

"You want me to be some sort of an intercessor?" she asked at last, clinging to the one thread she could unravel from his words. "A go-between for you and God?"

"I guess. If that's what you call it." He sighed. "I don't know. I need to learn how to redeem myself, how to get Him to make me whole, get back my control. If that's even possible." His face tightened. "I finally realized how much I need God, Gin. And now He's gone."

"But—why me, Tuck? Why do you need me?"

He grinned, the doubts slipping away in one moment of pure certainty.

"Because you're the only person I know who has her head on straight when it comes to God. You know, you've always known exactly how to talk to Him, how to ask for things, how to get your prayers answered."

She frowned, almost ready to tell him of her own doubts about a future she'd counted on for so long—a future with him. He stopped her cold with his next words.

"This doesn't have anything to do with what I said seven years ago. I know I promised I'd marry you, Gin.

At the time, I meant it. I would have liked to be your husband, believe me. But I can't do it, not now. I don't want or need a wife. Not knowing what I know.''

Somehow she scraped enough courage together to ask.

"What do you know, Tucker?"

The pain was there again, in full force, carving the lines in his face, draining away the hope that had once shone so brightly. Ginny shivered.

He shook his head at her, his face lined and tired.

"I can't love anyone, Gin. Not anyone. That's what God has taken away.''

She frowned, opened her mouth, but Tucker kept speaking.

"It's His form of justice, you see. I pushed too hard, didn't care enough about anyone but myself. So now He's made it so that I can never, ever love another person again.''

"What—"

"I'm incapable of love, Ginny. That's why I'll never marry anyone. I'd only hurt them—you.''

Ginny's eyes filled with tears as the terrible words sank through to her heart, killing her dream. He didn't want her as his wife, didn't need her to love him, care for him.

Tucker Townsend had come back to Jubilee Junction to ask Ginny to intercede for him with God, not to make her his bride.

Chapter Three

Two weeks later Ginny glared at herself in her bedroom mirror and prayed for deliverance from the chaos of her life.

A couple of things made her life a private misery. The worst was that Ginny couldn't make Tucker understand that she didn't have the resources she was certain he needed to help him break free of the guilt he was under.

They'd spent days talking, and Tucker still wouldn't accept the truth she'd offered—that he had to deal with God one-on-one. Tucker had some strange idea that Ginny was wired into heaven on a private line he expected her to use on his behalf. She'd urged him to seek counsel from someone trained to advise. She tried to steer him toward her pastor.

Tucker would have none of it. It was her or no one at all. The whole town wasn't going to know his problems, he insisted. He wouldn't talk to anyone else. And with every day that passed he seemed to slump deeper into his private abyss, so that now his agonized looks filled her dreams.

Second, Ginny knew she had to turn down the only marriage proposal she might ever receive. But two weeks of telephone messages left on an impersonal machine had kept her from telling Riley she couldn't marry him. She knew he'd just returned from a cattle auction five hundred miles away. She had a hunch his leaving had more to do with giving her time to think things over than with his need for more steers. She had used that time to consider everything and eventually acknowledged the truth. Riley wasn't madly in love with her. His proposal stemmed from something other than love.

She stared at the phone clutched in her hand. Time to clear this up. She prayed for tact.

"Hey, stranger. I've been trying to reach you."

"Hey, Ginny. I just got in and heard your messages."

The question hung between them. She knew he wouldn't ask again. It was up to her.

"I wanted to let you know my decision, Riley. I didn't like to keep you waiting."

"Uh-oh. It doesn't sound good."

"I'm very flattered that you would ask, but I'm sorry, I can't accept your proposal." Ginny rushed to reassure him. "I couldn't help wondering what made you ask. I'm pretty sure you only proposed that night because Tucker was back."

Silence. Then a sigh that told her she was right.

"Maybe just pushed it ahead a little, Ginny," Riley mumbled. "Once I come to a decision, I don't change my mind. I'd thought of it before then."

"But not seriously. I think you only offered to make sure I wasn't hurt." She hated this. "You didn't believe

Tucker had come back to marry me and you thought I'd be devastated, so you tried to protect me.''

''Yes, well, he didn't act like a man who was returning to the woman he loved.'' The gruff voice rasped the words out.

She felt such a wealth of tenderness then. Friends like this were hard to come by. She didn't want to lose Riley's friendship. After all, he was a friend who'd gone to great lengths to protect her.

''You were trying to shield me from the truth. I appreciate it, but it's not necessary, Riley. I'm a big girl. Tucker's been gone a long time.'' She forced herself to say the words, even though it hurt. ''He'll probably be gone again in a few days. I'll deal with it.''

''Has he said he's leaving?'' Riley demanded, his voice sharp.

''Not in actual words.'' Ginny shrugged away the memory. ''He said he can't feel love, not for anyone. He claims he's done something so terrible that God won't forgive him.'' She hid the hurt deep inside under a carefree attitude. ''He doesn't want a wife, he wants some kind of intercessor.''

''And you're telling me you're okay with that relationship?'' Riley sounded skeptical.

''I'll help him if I can. That's what friends do.'' She grinned. ''And you know all about that. Right, friend?''

''Yeah, I know.'' He laughed, not even bothering to conceal his relief.

''Thank you.'' His kindness still overwhelmed her.

''Anytime, pal. I didn't think you'd take me up on it, you know, Ginny. In fact, that's why I signed up for the rodeo circuit down south. I knew you wouldn't. I'll be gone for the next few months.''

Ginny heard the concern behind his voice.

"I'll be fine, Riley. But you take care. You've been such a good friend to me. Don't get hurt at the rodeo, will you?"

"Nah." He waited a moment, then spoke again, his voice brimming with quiet concern. "Don't get hurt too much helping Tucker. He's not the same guy he was in high school, Ginny."

"I know." She shifted, squeezing her eyes closed to block the tears. "Believe me, I know."

"Bye, Ginny."

"Goodbye, Riley."

She hung the phone up slowly, catching a glimpse of herself in the mirror as she did.

"You are a first-class idiot," she informed the disheveled woman who stared at her. "How can you be so stupid as to sit around and wait for a guy who hasn't given you the time of day in seven years?"

The idiot stared back, eyes dropping to the picture that sat on the edge of her dresser. Tucker.

"Why can't you find someone else to stare at?"

"Did you say something to me, honey?" Her father leaned in the doorway, his eyes approving her black jeans and bright orange sweater.

"No, sorry, Dad. Just talking to myself. Again." She leaned down to tug on a pair of socks, then laced on her battered leather boots. Tucker's snarky comment about her shoes made her only too aware of his scrutiny.

"Is there a problem? Anything I can do to help?"

"Thanks anyway, Dad, but I've gotten myself into this mess. I think I'll just have to clean it up myself." Ginny stood on tiptoe to brush her lips against his balding pate.

She'd barely started down the steps when his words halted her.

"It's that boy, isn't it? The Townsend boy. He still hasn't worked out what he's after."

"Well, he isn't after me, that's for sure. But he has got problems." Ginny stepped more slowly down the remaining risers, her mind searching for an answer. She didn't want her dad worrying about her problems, especially not if they had to do with Tucker.

"What's he got problems with?" Her father followed her into the den and sank into his favorite chair while she curled up on the love seat. "His injuries aren't healing?"

"He's got other injuries, Dad. Deeper ones. He's asked me to help him sort through them."

"And?"

"I've tried to steer him to someone stronger, someone with more knowledge." She stared at her fingernails, searching for the right words. "There's a desperation about him now, Dad. I don't like it. It scares me. He's tortured within his mind."

"Is it something about his friend dying?"

Ginny's head jerked up. "How did you know?"

Her father smiled. "It's what sent him back here, isn't it? Even I can deduce that much. I'm sick, Virginia, not senile."

"I didn't mean that, Dad, and you know it." She sighed. "The whole thing is just so difficult. What am I supposed to say, to do? I barely know Tucker anymore."

"Maybe you don't have to say anything. Maybe you just have to listen."

Ginny gulped. "You mean—you *want* me to do this?"

"I told you, I think you're probably the only one who can help him out. I don't know why I think that, but I do. The other day I saw him. He was sitting by himself in the park. You know, Tuesday, I think it was.''

Ginny nodded. The unseasonably warm spring days were a blessing they all enjoyed.

"Tucker didn't even seem to notice the weather. He was off in some bleak, cold place his mind carried him to. His eyes were glazed, and when I called out, it took him a long time to come back from wherever he was. It scared me, I'll tell you.''

"Why?''

"I've only ever seen something like that once before.'' Her father shook his head sadly. "My older brother, Mel, served in Vietnam. When he came back, he retreated and retreated from the rest of us. He dreamed horrible things that tortured him until he was afraid to close his eyes.''

"I've never heard you mention this before.'' Ginny saw his sadness. "Is this the brother that died?''

"Yes.'' Her father nodded, his face pale. "He came home from work one day, told us all he had to go away. He said he loved us, but he couldn't stay. Then he drove his car over an embankment. I guess it was the only way he knew to stop the pain.''

Aghast, Ginny stared at her father. "But if Tucker's suffering like that, I'm in no way qualified to help him!''

"Qualifications don't matter in this case, honey. He's chosen you. All he wants is for you to be there for him. Who else has he got?''

She sighed.

Her father nodded. "I've spent years in that store, and a lot of my time's been spent listening. Nine times out of ten, that's all anybody wants—somebody to listen to them. It's as if once they dump out their problems, they can sort through them and gain a new perspective. It doesn't take psychiatric training to listen.''

''I guess it can't hurt,'' she muttered, only half-believing her own words. ''I just hope you're right. Tucker hasn't exactly opened up to anyone around here. He locks himself away in his own little world and broods. I don't really know why he came back here at all.'' Ginny got up, straightened her clothes. ''I'd better get going.''

''He'll talk when he's ready. Just be there.'' The phone rang. Her father jerked his head toward the telephone. ''That's probably him now. He's called at least four times in the past couple of hours. I tried to tell him you had a consultation and then you were going to the church, but I don't think he heard me.''

''Don't feel bad. He ignores a lot of what I say, too.'' Ginny picked up the phone. ''Hello? Hi, Tucker.'' She listened for a moment, then shook her head. ''I'm sorry, I can't. I have a meeting. At the church.''

''Oh,'' Tucker said. Then there was dead silence.

She looked at her father. Adrian raised one eyebrow and nodded.

''Ask him,'' he mouthed.

''Why don't you come? It's because of you that we're doing this fund-raiser, you know.'' Ginny quickly told Tucker about the night she'd seen his report on the orphanage and the lack of fresh water in the war-torn country.

''We decided to see if we could raise enough money to pay for a well. All because of you.'' She thought for a second, then plunged on. ''Please come, just this first night. Lend your support? Maybe you could say a few words afterward to help us understand the best way to help.''

He didn't speak for a long time, then muttered his answer. Ginny listened, nodded, grinned and hung up the phone.

"Maybe." She crossed both fingers. "At least he didn't say no."

"Worth a try." Her father padded along on his slippered feet, following her to the front door. "He needs to get out."

"You'll be all right, won't you, Dad? This first meeting isn't all that important. We're just hoping we get people on board to help us raise enough funds. I can stay if you need me."

"Go. I'll be fine. Besides, I think you need to be there. I told Tucker about your project, you know."

"You did? He didn't say anything." She searched her father's face. "Why did you tell him?"

Her father avoided her stare. "I, uh, I thought he needed to know his work had done some good."

"Uh-huh." She peered at him. "And?"

Her father's chest huffed out belligerently. "I had to do my part, Virginia. He won't come to church, avoids everyone on coffee row. He even refused to help Coach with the football games." His face filled with pity. "Mrs. Bains says he sits in his room most of the time, staring at the walls."

"All right, Dad. I'll make an effort to get him to talk tonight. If he comes." She waited for his nod. "But I'm only doing it on one condition."

"A condition? Uh—" Adrian turned away "—I think I heard the phone."

"No, you did not." She shook her head, wrapping her fingers around his wrist to stop him from escaping. "Come on, Dad. Just promise me you'll eat all that salad I made, and at least half of the puny little casserole in the oven. Agreed?''

"Ginny, I'm not really hungry these days.''

"Deal?'' she demanded, glaring at him.

"Yes. All right. It's a deal. You are such a bossy daughter.'' He sighed, hustled her out the door, then slammed it closed behind her.

Ginny grinned. At least she'd scored one victory for the home team. Now to deal with Tucker.

By the time Ginny arrived at the church, most of the adult fellowship group was there, laughing and chattering as they greeted each other.

In the middle of Rob Lassiter's joke about grooms, Tucker rode into the parking lot on his motorcycle. Several long anxious moments passed as she waited for him to come in. But Tucker never appeared. The pastor clapped his hands to get their attention.

"We're ready to begin, folks. If you'd all take a seat.''

Ginny waited until the foyer was empty. Would Tucker come in, or would he run away?

Finally he walked through the door.

"Hi, Tucker. I'm glad you came. They're just about to start, so you haven't missed a thing.'' She heard herself chattering madly, but she couldn't seem to stop. This was the first effort he'd made to be part of their group.

She pointed out some empty chairs near the back of the fellowship hall. "How about here?''

"It's fine.'' He waited until she was seated, then flopped down beside her.

"Looks like a good turnout, don't you think? After they watch the clip, everyone is going to contribute ideas, and we're going to have a contest for the most successful ones.'' She smiled at him, trying to ease his obvious discomfort. "It won't be a very long meeting."

"You sure I won't be intruding?" Tucker glanced furtively around the room as the lights dimmed. "I hardly know anyone."

Ginny thought he resembled a street person. His hair stood out in shaggy tufts. His eyes were bleary, his clothes rumpled. Her heart ached at the sight of the once-fastidious reporter.

"Of course you're not intruding. I was just trying to come up with some ideas of my own for the fund-raiser."

"Uh-huh." Tucker slumped beside her.

"We're hoping to get enough to dig a really good well. African famines and dry spells are notorious." Babbling again. Ginny clamped her lips together and prayed.

Finally Tucker's recorded news presentation started. Only then did she wonder if this would remind him too much of the past.

"Please, God. Help him," she whispered. She focused on the plight of children dying in a world where water was worth its weight in gold.

Ginny wasn't sure how much time elapsed before she noticed Tucker's unease. But gradually her attention was diverted by his shuffling foot, his fidgeting body, his hissing breath as another display of human brutality flew across the screen, underscored by his quiet, solemn voice. She had to do something.

Ginny reached out and touched his arm. "It's hard to look at, isn't it? I've never understood why people are like that."

Tucker jerked his head once in affirmation. His eyes

flickered over her face before they were drawn to the screen by the mournful wails of a family bereft of its father.

Ginny, who'd previewed the video, remembered well the graphic scenes. The pastor hadn't been sure how his congregation would react, but the plight of these people was so horrible, so hopeless, that the committee had decided the shock value for comfortable North Americans might be good.

Apparently he'd been wrong.

With at least four minutes of tape still remaining, Tucker bolted from the room, his departure so noisy many of the others turned to see what was wrong.

"What happened to him, Ginny?" Rob Lassiter turned in his seat as he watched Tucker shove the door open and almost run outside.

"I don't know, Rob. Maybe he remembers someone he visited in this place. Maybe it brings back memories he'd rather not have." Why had she asked him here tonight?

"He's a reporter. He covered the story." Rob frowned. "Surely he can't be all that affected by it now?"

Ginny barely heard him. Her eyes stung. She recalled the ravaged look on Tucker's face as he'd opened the door. The light had sparkled off the tears coursing down his cheeks.

What on earth was wrong with him?

The pictures died away, and the chairman got up to speak. Ginny slipped out the door as soundlessly as she could.

"Where did he go?" Ginny scoured the parking lot, but saw nothing. "Tucker?"

She stood perfectly still, her ears attuned to the night

sounds of the little town. After a minute she walked around the corner of the church.

Tucker was there, his face pressed against the cold brick wall as he gasped for breath.

Ginny touched his shoulder, felt the trembling that shivered through his muscles.

"Tucker? Are you all right?"

"Fine." His brusque tone belied his words.

"I'm sorry. It was pretty horrific stuff."

"No worse than a lot of places. You can go back in. I'm fine. Just needed a breath of air." The gruff words came out raw, needy.

"I don't have to go back. I already know what comes next. I'm on the committee." She sensed he didn't want her to see him like this, so Ginny pretended to concentrate on scuffing her toe against the sidewalk. "If you need anything—"

"I don't." Tucker shoved himself away from the wall and glared at her. "I'm perfectly fine. You don't have to hover around here like some nursemaid for a puny child, or a mother with a baby chick, Gin. I wanted some air—I took a walk. End of story."

But his eyes, when he stepped under the floodlight, were not those of a man who was out for his constitutional. They were the eyes of a man who'd seen too much.

"I don't mind missing the chitchat," Ginny told him quietly. "If I know Vera Malloy, the ideas will be getting pretty outlandish right about now. She sometimes gets carried away."

"I don't need a baby-sitter!" Tucker's voice dropped to a whisper as some of the men began to leave the church. "You said you can't help me. Fine. I accept that. I won't bother you any more."

Ginny frowned. What brought this on?

"I'm your friend, Tucker. I'm concerned about you."

"I don't want your *concern!* I asked you for help. You won't do it. Okay. I accept that."

"I didn't say I wouldn't, I just said I don't know how." Frustration made her voice sharper than she intended. Ginny softened it. "I'm sorry."

"Just leave me alone," he said bitterly.

"I can't. What do you want from me, Tucker? You won't talk to me, you won't come to the house, won't stay after church, won't join in with anything, but you claim I'm supposed to help you. How? I don't even know what's wrong with you! You've got to stop hiding. You've got to let me in."

The others poured from the building. They stood in groups discussing ways and means of funding a new well for those who so badly needed it.

"That was some journalism, Tucker. We're going to the coffee shop to plan some team strategy. Wanna join us?"

Tucker half-turned away from Ginny, his voice slightly muffled. "No, thanks, anyway. I think I'll just head on home and get some of Mrs. Bains's hot chocolate."

"She always did coddle you the most."

The rest of the group joined in with remarks meant to make Tucker feel like he'd come home and also to lighten the atmosphere. Now that they knew the scope of the horror, they needed to concentrate on alleviating it. Dwelling on the negative wouldn't help.

Ginny suspected it cost Tucker a great deal not to turn away when the focus was turned on him by an old school buddy.

"Nice to see you out, Tucker. Feels pretty good to

be back home in Jubilee, huh?'' One eyebrow lifted suggestively. "You wanna pitch in with us? Your past experience should be good for something.''

Ginny gasped as her stomach hit her toes. She watched Tucker straighten, saw him mask his distress. He strolled over to his motorbike, ignoring her outstretched hand.

"You'd think so, Wolf, wouldn't you? You'd certainly think so.''

Tucker pulled on his helmet, completely ignoring Ginny when she followed him to the bike. She stood waiting as he snapped the strap, hoping he'd speak. Between the poor lighting and the darkness of his visor, she couldn't read his expression, couldn't tell how the words were affecting him.

"He didn't mean anything, Tucker," she whispered, touching his hand. "He was just trying to include you.''

"Yeah. I know.'' He yanked his hand away, pulled on his gloves and revved the motor. His fingers clenched the grips. "The funny thing is, he's right. All those years of covering that misery should be put to use. I guess I'll just have to think on that.'' Then he flicked her a nod. "Good night, Ginny.''

He was gone with a quiet roar that spoke more loudly than anything he'd said. Ginny peered after him worriedly.

It wasn't the words that bothered her. Tucker had always had lots of words. It was the way he'd said them—hopelessly, listlessly, as if he were finished trying to figure everything out.

In an echo of memory, her father's words about his brother played over in her mind. She shivered.

Please, God, just keep Tucker safe tonight. Hold him

tight in the hollow of Your hand, and don't let go. I promise I'll talk to him again tomorrow, Lord. I'll do whatever he needs of me. I'll find a way to be what he needs. Just keep Tucker Townsend safe tonight.

Chapter Four

Tucker wheeled his bike into Ginny's driveway and flicked off the motor, conscious of the group of rowdy boys who'd been dogging him for the past four blocks. He'd hoped they'd give up, but apparently such hopes were futile. He knew from past experience that a motorbike drew teenage boys as well or better than a burger and fries.

This gang was no different.

He stayed exactly where he was, hoping he hadn't brought trouble to the Browns. He'd seen these kids hanging around town. He'd know the type anywhere. Bored, with a negative attitude, they were trouble just waiting to happen. He'd have to watch what he said.

They dropped their bicycles on the Browns' lawn and clustered around him, five boys, thirteen, fourteen, maybe fifteen, with scraggly hair and scruffy clothes. The message in their slow swaggers didn't need translating. They were bad boys, and proud of it.

Tucker lifted his visor, nodded. "Hey."

"Hey, yourself." One of them, probably the ringleader, jerked a finger toward the bike as if ordering Tucker off. "I wanna try."

"Sorry. Nobody touches Betty but me."

"Betty?" They hooted with derisive laughter.

Tucker pretended to ignore them. According to Coach, these kids had caused a lot of problems around town with their open defiance. Most of it happened at night, when these juvenile offenders were supposed to be at home, in bed. He'd better watch his back.

"Yeah, Betty. She's brand-new off the line." He began listing mechanical statistics by rote. They probably didn't know anything about bikes, but at least they were quiet.

"Not bad." One of the kids uttered a low whistle of appreciation as his hand stroked the shiny black metal. "She's a beauty. When did you get her?"

"A couple of weeks ago. It was one of the first things I bought after I got out of the hospital."

"You cracked up?"

"No." Tucker offered minimal information about the injuries he'd sustained. "Once I was okayed for driving, I could hardly wait to get out on the open road."

"Yeah. Freedom, man." The carrot-headed boy jerked his head as if he totally understood. "That's cool. Me, I'm not going to report to anyone. When I make eighteen, I'll hit the road and be my own boss. No more rules."

"There are always rules." Who knew that better than him? Tucker unsnapped his helmet and pulled it off. "You can't get away from them. What's your name?"

"Tom." The boy huffed, glancing around his to see the impact of his words on the others. "You can always get away from the rules, man. You just do your own thing and ignore everybody else. Forget all the dos and don'ts.''

''Might work on a desert island,'' Tucker agreed, ''but it doesn't sound like much of a life to me.''

''Aw, what do you know?'' Tom kicked the front tire of the bike. ''You've probably been living in this hick town all your life. I'll bet you never drive more than five miles outside this hillbilly town when you crank this thing up.'' He turned away, motioning to the others. ''C'mon, guys, this hotshot's a deadbeat.''

''Actually,'' Tucker muttered, ''I know exactly what I'm talking about. This is the first time I've been back to Jubilee Junction in seven years.'' Why had he let them con that out of him?

''Oh, yeah?'' Tom turned around, interest flickering through eyes that pretended bravado. ''Where you been?''

''Lots of places.'' Tucker told them about his job.

''You don't look famous to me.'' Tom's bottom lip curled. ''No way you're a celebrity.''

''I didn't say I was famous.'' Tucker flopped down on the grass. If nothing else, these kids were good for keeping his ego in check. ''How many news programs do you watch, Tom?''

''None. Dead boring bunch of garbage.'' He hunkered down beside Tucker and snicked a piece of grass to shove between his teeth. ''The guy I'm staying with, he's big into that stuff. Runs the newspaper.''

''Marty Owens. I know him. Runs a good paper.'' Marty was sixty if he was a day and had never looked after a kid in his life. The newspaper was his baby. ''How come you're staying with Marty?''

Tom's slight shoulders jerked back in a defensive

stance. He glared at Tucker. "Why'd you want to know?"

"Just wondered. You have something to hide?"

The other boys lunged onto the grass, too, their grins teasing.

"If he does, he blew it. Tom's fires aren't exactly a secret."

Tucker watched as Tom clenched his lips. The boy ignored the others. He stared straight ahead. When he spoke, his voice was tight, barely controlled.

"I'm doing them a favor, see? Mr. Owens needs money, so he said he'd be a foster father. I got picked to be the guinea pig for some new program the legal system thinks will turn me into an angel." He smirked as one thumb jerked over his shoulder. "We all did. Lucky us."

The other boys added their comments as the front door of the house squeaked open. Tucker turned. Ginny stood on the threshold, her eyes wide as she took in the motley group.

"Hi, Tucker. Friends of yours?"

Tucker wanted to shout with laughter. That was Ginny. She took everything in stride—even six punky-looking kids.

"We just met," he told her, grinning.

"Hey, lady, what's that smell?" Tom twisted to better catch the aroma wafting from the house.

"Chocolate brownies," Tucker told him, his nose twitching. "With peanut butter fudge icing." He closed his eyes and let the sensations overwhelm him. How many times had Ginny cooked his favorite treat in the old days?

"I just took them out of the oven. They're for dessert."

Tucker opened his eyes in time to see the kid next to Tom nudge his neighbor.

"Chocolate brownies," he whispered in awe.

Tucker hid his smile, but it wasn't easy. "How long have you lived here, Tom?"

The kid's eyes narrowed with suspicion.

"I'm serious. A couple of days?"

"Two months," Tom blurted. "Why?"

"You've been here two months and you never found out about Ginny's brownies?" Tucker shook his head. "Sad, really sad. You guys have no idea what you've missed."

Every single boy licked his lips.

"They're that good?" one squeaked in a voice that puberty was altering.

"Better," Tucker told him seriously.

"I was just going to put some burgers on the grill," Ginny murmured. "Would your friends like to join us?"

Since she'd invited him over for a fried fish dinner, Tucker figured she'd deliberately changed the menu. He didn't know why, exactly, but she'd lived here longer. Maybe she knew something he didn't. He'd go with her instincts.

Tucker studied the bunch of them. "You guys up for some burgers?"

They all nodded, except for Tom.

"Burgers *and* brownies?" he demanded, his eyes on Ginny.

She shrugged. "Sure, if you want. I'm allergic to chocolate, and Dad can't have it. I only made them for Tucker."

"I guess I could eat something." Tom lurched to his feet and sauntered toward the door.

Tucker had to hurry to beat him. He planted himself in the middle of the doorframe, beside Ginny, and stared. Tom stared right back.

"Thank you," he said softly.

"Huh?" Tom pretended he hadn't understood, but the flush on his cheeks gave him away. "What're you talking about?"

"It's customary to say thank-you when someone invites you to eat with them." Tucker crossed his arms over his chest and waited, sincerely hoping they wouldn't test him on this. He was feeling better than he had in weeks, but no way could he protect Ginny if push came to shove.

A hiss of frustration emanated from the redhead's lips. "Yeah, sure. Thanks." Tom thrust his chin out defiantly.

"You're welcome. Now, come on in." Ginny tugged on Tucker's arm, nudging him out of the way. "The phone's over there. You guys need to call home and ask permission to stay. Then we'll start grilling. Tucker, you come with me."

She practically dragged him into the kitchen, her fingernails poking into his arm.

"Take it easy with those nails," he told her, rubbing the spot. "They'll probably steal something, you know. I can't imagine why you invited them in. We were supposed to talk."

"Sorry." She smiled. "I didn't mean to hurt you. I was just trying to get you out of the way." She handed him a packet of matches. "We will talk."

"I mean to each other. You promised to help me, remember?" Tucker sighed when Ginny opened the back door and pointed to the barbecue.

"Light it, please," she said, then turned to pull a

packet of burgers from the freezer. When he didn't move, she sighed, stopped what she was doing and faced him. "We'll talk, Tucker. I promised to help if I could, and I will. I just thought it would be nice if those kids joined us. I don't expect it's easy being an outcast."

"Is that what they are?" He walked out the patio door, lit the barbecue and closed the lid so it would heat up. "Your dad's not going to be impressed."

Ginny glanced at him through the kitchen window and grinned. Tucker walked inside.

"He'll love it. We don't have enough company." Her hands moved in a flash, slicing tomatoes, setting cheese slices, pickles and lettuce on a platter. "Mustard, ketchup and relish I've got," she murmured. "What about onions?"

"I hate onions." Tom sauntered through the doorway, his face drawn into the hard lines he used to show his toughness. "And you better not give him any." He jerked a thumb at Tucker.

"Why not?" Tucker demanded. "I like onions on my burger."

"Maybe she doesn't like kissing onion breath." Tom grinned at their shocked looks, then nudged his snickering friends.

Tucker fumed. For two cents he'd send them home—without burgers. But one look at Ginny and he reconsidered. She was laughing.

"Nice one, Tom. You think fast on your feet. I bet you're a whiz at school." She handed him the platter of burgers. "You can go and start these if you want. Just don't let them burn. I don't eat charcoal. Here, guys, there's something for each of you. Picnic table's on the deck through that door. Put everything out there.''

They did as she asked, toting out plates, glasses and condiments like obedient soldiers.

''We're lucky it's turned so warm.'' She emptied frozen orange juice into a pitcher and mixed it with water. ''Eating outside makes things taste so much better.''

''He has the wrong idea, Gin.'' Tucker had to say it to clarify that he wasn't nursing any romantic intentions toward her. He didn't want to hurt her, but he didn't want to leave expectations he couldn't fulfill, either.

She whirled, hair tumbling over her shoulders in a riot of curls. As usual when she was ticked at him, Ginny couldn't hide the glint in those emerald-green eyes. Tucker shifted from one foot to the other. Didn't she know he didn't want to hurt her?

''Fine. He has the wrong idea. I know the truth. So do you. Isn't that what's important?'' She sighed. ''They're teenagers, Tuck. They're trying to get your goat. Will you please relax?''

''I just didn't want…''

''Me to harbor any illusions about your motives for being here,'' she finished. ''I've got it, okay? I understand, Tucker.''

Tucker thought her eyes misted over, but there was nothing misty about her voice. It was calm, steady and a little angry.

''Don't believe me, huh? All right, then. How about this—we're not getting married, you don't love me, you can never love me because love is something you're fresh out of. There, does that about cover the issue?''

Without waiting for his response, she grabbed the juice and stomped out the door. Tucker called himself a fool in three different African dialects before he joined her outside. Maybe he hadn't *wanted* to hurt her, but it seemed as if he was doing just that.

"You're back, I see," said Ginny's father. Adrian Brown sat on a lounger, his glasses perched on the end of his nose, the local newspaper spread across his lap.

"Yeah, I'm back. I hope it's okay. The kids just sort of showed up." He probably should have asked her dad if it was okay before he let Ginny drag the boys in to eat them out of house and home, Tucker told himself.

"I'm glad they came." Adrian grinned. "I like to think they can come here. They need a stabilizing influence." He smiled, his eyes on Ginny as she chucked a football to Tom. Her toss easily covered the length of the huge backyard. "Would you mind checking those burgers? I get indigestion from burned food."

Tucker checked, then sank beside Ginny's father in a white chair.

"I guess you noticed that I hurt her again," he muttered. "I can't seem to stop doing that."

"I heard your conversation." Adrian shrugged. "It might be an idea to stop rehashing the past. Forget it. Pretend you've only known each other for a little while."

"That's kind of hard to do. I did promise I'd come back and marry her." He waited for the anger.

"Yeah, you did promise. And you broke it. She understands. Just give it some time to sink in." Adrian shifted uncomfortably.

"Are you all right?" Tucker couldn't believe how much the man had aged.

"I'm fine. It's just frustrating when they can't figure out what's wrong with me. I have to go back for tests again."

"I'm sorry." Tucker didn't know what else to say.

Adrian Brown had always been robust, healthy and active. Tucker knew exactly how awful it was to lose your health. "Ginny and I were supposed to talk tonight."

"I know. She's been looking up some scriptures she thought might help you." Adrian pointed at the grill. "That's a lot of smoke."

Tucker had barely lifted the lid when Ginny came racing up and grabbed the lifter.

"Come on, guys. Dad, this is Tom, Paul, Nick, Ira, John and Kent. Boys, my dad." She squinted at the grill. "These burgers are charbroiled." She laid them on the buns, saving the darkest, most burned one for Tucker. "I assume this is the way you like them, since you let them burn," she teased, handing it over.

He took it, loaded on the condiments and bit into it.

"Of course," he mumbled, his mouth full. "Kills all the bacteria."

"Now why didn't I think of that." She picked the black spots off the edges of her burger and flopped it into a bun.

"You couldn't." He grinned at the surprised look on her face. "It's a guy thing, Gin. Girls don't get it."

Tom and his friends let out huge guffaws, clearly enjoying their repartee. Tucker watched them, a small pain pinching his heart. What did it feel like to be so carefree? How long since he'd laughed for the sheer pleasure of enjoying life?

Too long. Some of his tenseness ebbed away as Tucker relaxed and ate his burger. *Let go of it,* he ordered his brain.

Ginny's brownies were a hit, as usual. Decadent squares of rich dark chocolate disappeared like grain before locusts until not a smear of icing was left on the plate.

"If only I'd known," Tom moaned, clasping his hand to his stomach. "I'd have been here weeks ago."

"There are lots of things you don't know about this place." Tucker swallowed the last glob of icing. "You have to take more interest in the town, get to know the real Jubilee Junction."

Tom nodded. "You think?" he said, but his voice was thoughtful rather than snide.

The boys stayed almost three hours. Once they'd finished eating, they helped clean up, then played a game of tag football. It wasn't long before Tom discovered the stand of maple trees near the back of the lot and climbed up the sturdy branches.

"Hey, you've got your own river," Tom shouted to Ginny from his perch high atop the biggest tree.

"I'd forgotten that!" Tucker left the deck and strode across the grass until he came to the pebbled shore. His and Ginny's favorite haunt.

It looked exactly the same.

The boys followed one by one, curiosity drawing them. As usual, Tom was in the lead.

"Look at the fog over that pool. Cool."

"No, it's actually warm," Tucker explained. "There's a geothermal spring underneath that heats it up all year."

"Even in the winter?" They stared at him, their disbelief evident.

"Uh-huh. Temperature varies a little, depending on the rainfall, but we've sat in there on Christmas eve with snow all around and been warm as toast." Tucker remembered that last Christmas so vividly.

"Way cool," Tom murmured. "Your own private hot tub!"

Ginny's shout from the deck drew their attention.

Curfew. It was time to go. Tucker stood silent as each boy thanked Ginny and her father for the evening.

"I'm glad you came," she told them sincerely. "We'll do it again. Soon."

"You mean it?" Tom's disbelief was evident.

"Of course."

"When?" he challenged.

"I'm not exactly sure. Dad has to go to the city for some tests, so everything's a little mixed up right now." She patted her father on the shoulder. "But we'll get it straightened out."

"I didn't know you were sick. I'm sorry we bothered you."

Tom's sincere concern touched Tucker. The boy was capable of more than the thug image he cultivated. Too bad he made it so difficult to get past the facade.

"You didn't bother me, son. I enjoyed having you and your friends here. Reminded me of when Tucker used to come over." Adrian grinned. "He always hogged the brownies, too. Even tried to sneak them home."

Tom glanced once at his jacket pocket. His face darkened to a vivid beet red.

"It's okay, son. I understand. I used to filch them when Ginny's mom made them years ago." Adrian smiled at the memory. "I missed them after she died."

Tom shuffled from one foot to the other. The rest of the gang had left. He was the last one, and he clearly felt out of place. But it was obvious that he had something to say.

"I don't know if you'd want me to come back if you knew about me," he muttered finally, his eyes on Tucker.

"Knew what, son?" Adrian Brown stayed exactly where he was, his body relaxed, his smile firmly in place.

Uh-oh. Tucker's mind clicked into high gear. Fire, he remembered. Some kid had talked about Tom's fires. Probation. Prickles of fear zapped along the hair on his arms. Maybe he really had endangered the Browns.

"I used to light fires." Tom glared at Tucker, daring him to say something. "I'm not a pyromaniac or anything, but I got into trouble a lot. They sent me to live with my mom in Billings, but I got in trouble again. The Owens were starting this program, and they offered to take kids in trouble, so the judge sent me here. If I mess up again, I have to go to jail." He lifted his head, his blue eyes hard. "I don't care."

"That's not true. Of course you care. You'd have to be an idiot not to. And you're not an idiot, Tom. Not the way your mind works." Adrian laid his head back against his chair and closed his eyes.

"You mean it?" Tom glanced from Adrian to Tucker.

"I mean it." Adrian smiled. "You're welcome here, Tom. Anytime. Good night."

Thus dismissed, Tom could do nothing but mutter good-night and leave. Once he was gone, Tucker turned toward Adrian, prepared to ask him not to see the kid again. But Ginny's hand on his arm stopped him. She shook her head, eyes asking him to remain silent. A minute later Tucker knew why.

"Bedtime, Dad. You're almost sleeping in that chair." Her voice emerged soft and light.

"I am rather tired. Must be the fresh air and the excitement of those kids." Adrian got to his feet. "Full of energy, that bunch. Need a little direction, though." He stretched and sighed.

"Spring's a wonderful time. New beginnings, fresh starts. Nothing like it for building faith in the future." He leaned over to kiss Ginny's forehead. "Good night, honey."

"Good night, Dad. Sleep well." She hugged him tightly.

Only Tucker saw the pain flicker across her face as her father shuffled slowly into the house.

"Was it too much? I could have sent them home sooner."

"He's fine, Tucker." She smiled and shook her head. "But he's right. Those boys do need something to do. With the whole summer looming before them, it's just asking for trouble to let them run loose." She yawned, then turned to peer through the gloom at him. "You've been quiet. What are you thinking?"

"About how much things have changed."

"And maybe how much they've stayed the same?" She sat in her father's lounger, eyes cast upward. "It's the same moon, the same stars. The same God who never changes, no matter what we think."

"Actually I was thinking of what your dad said— beginnings." Tucker retreated to his own chair. "We never realize how precious beginnings are and yet we only get them once."

"That's where you're wrong, Tuck." She wiggled, trying to find a comfortable position. "God's mercies are new every morning. When we admit our sin, He wipes it out, and we get to start all over again. He gives us new days, new months, new years over and over. Every moment, every hour is fresh and new, never used before."

He smiled. That was Ginny, optimistic to the end.

"I wish I had a whole new life," he thought, unaware he'd said the words aloud.

"What do you mean?"

Tucker mocked himself for even pretending he could start over. The real truth was he envied those kids their future.

"I'd like to shed this horrible existence and start all over again, fresh and clean. Without the scars."

She glanced at his eye. "Is it bothering you?"

"No. But I meant without the mental scars."

"No way!" Ginny sat up straight. "That's how I figure out the future, by looking at the past."

"Huh?"

"Remember when I decided to become a ballerina?"

Tucker almost choked trying to stifle the laughter.

"Vaguely," he finally managed to say.

"Oh, give it up, Tucker. Laugh if you want to. I know it was crazy." She ignored his boisterous chuckles. "I got fixated on those tutus, and that was it."

"At least you tried." She'd been so determined, he remembered. She'd insisted it was simply mind over matter.

"Boy, did I try! I spent hours trying."

Tucker was glad for the darkness. He could no longer hide his grin. She'd tripped over her point shoes, torn her tutu and scraped her elbows. Not to mention breaking just about every piece of glass her parents owned.

"No offense, Gin, but you're not exactly coordinated." He could still see her lunging and huffing as she tried to pirouette.

"Thanks a lot!" Her green eyes flashed a warning. "I think you can stop laughing at me now."

He picked up his glass and hid his smile behind it.

"Anyway—what I was trying to say was that I knew a dance career was out for me."

"I could have told you that." He snickered, enjoying her discomfiture. "On the first day."

It wasn't often anyone caught Ginny at a disadvantage. Tucker allowed himself a few seconds to relish her embarrassment. She was always so competent, so in control, but she wasn't perfect. It was a comfort knowing that.

"As I was saying," she continued, ignoring his interruption, "the experience did teach me that I enjoyed mixing and matching textures and colors. I'm pretty sure that's when I got hooked on fabrics."

"And now you design people's homes." He'd seen her work here and at Coach's house. She was very good at creating just the right atmosphere.

"Yes, but I didn't just float into it, you know. I had to experience something, fail at it and then move on. Even Jesus grew in wisdom. That's what life's all about, isn't it? Using our failures to grow?"

The question bothered Tucker. He forced himself to think it over analytically, refused to let himself get trapped by emotion.

"What would you suggest I'm supposed to learn from my experience?" Frustration chewed at him as the past welled up in his brain. "Don't get into the middle of someone else's conflict?"

"I don't know. Maybe." She sounded serious.

"Ginny, that's ridiculous! That's what reporters do."

"Is it?" She looped her long legs under her, elbows on her knees, face thoughtful.

"Of course it is. I want answers."

"I know. Believe me, I still hear echoes of you ask-

ing, 'Why, Mr. Brown?'" She winked at his embarrassed look.

"Haven't changed much, have you? Except these
days you want your answers now, because you're used
to thirty-second sound bites and quick decisions. Sometimes it just doesn't work that way, Tuck." She cupped
her chin in her palm.

He waited for her to continue, knowing she would
reach a point soon.

"I mean, just look at my dad. He's been suffering
for quite a while, hoping, waiting, trying to understand.
And while he waits, the doctors rule out first one thing,
then another."

"And he's no better off for it." Tucker hated saying
that, but it was the truth, and it knocked the stuffing out
of her argument.

"Of course he's better off for it!" Ginny scrunched
her forehead in thought. "What if some hotshot doctor
made a snap decision based on preliminary tests and
assumed Dad needed a quadruple bypass. So they go
ahead and do the surgery, he heals, but he's still no
better. What good is that?"

"What you're telling me is that I need to have patience?" He snorted. "I can't afford that."

"You can't afford not to."

She leaned over, her fingers on his sleeve. The
warmth penetrated the fabric to his skin, soothing his
fractured nerves. He shouldn't allow it, but Tucker
couldn't help enjoying that touch. Sometimes he even
thought he craved it.

"I know it isn't easy, Tucker, but maybe God is using
this experience to teach you something new. The Bible
says we have to search for God before He can be found.
Maybe that's what you have to do."

He twined his fingers in hers, linking their hands. It felt comfortable, familiar.

"But I *have* searched and I haven't found anything. I don't get a response. God doesn't hear me." Across the road the crickets started their chant. Tucker closed his eyes for a moment and let the old emotions roll off him.

"Did God hear you in the past?"

"Yes. Or at least, I thought so." He raked a hand through his hair. "I don't know. Everything's so confused. Maybe I just thought I had a relationship with God."

"Tucker." Ginny was out of her chair in a flash and kneeling in front of him. Her hands slid around his face, forcing him to look at her. "Close your eyes."

She waited until he obeyed.

"Good. Now, think back. Think about high school. Think about the Good Friday rallies, the Bible studies we held at the lake, the camping trips. Did you believe God heard you then?"

He nodded. The certainty of those memorable times was solid, secure.

"God doesn't change, Tuck. He's the same as He was yesterday. He'll be the same tomorrow."

Tucker opened his eyes and stared into the conviction of her shining green gaze. "But it's not the same. I don't feel anything."

"The feelings aren't what counts, Tucker. The truth is that He's there, and He's the same as He always was." She studied him seriously. "Maybe it's you who's changed."

"Maybe." He wasn't sure anymore.

Ginny was silent for several moments. When she spoke her voice was hesitant.

"Say something really important came up and I
wanted to contact my dad. I'd phone him. If he didn't
answer, I'd try again and again until I reached him."

He couldn't stop the half smile at her logic. "Maybe
he's moved or isn't answering the phone."

"Then I'd find that out. The point is, I want to talk
to my dad, and nothing's going to stop me."

"And that's what I have to do? Keep trying?" It
sounded slow and tedious.

Ginny lifted her hands away from his face, stood,
then stepped back and looked at him.

"Tucker, maybe this will hurt you. If it does, I'm
sorry, but I still have to say it." She took a deep, au-
dible breath. "You want God to come to you on your
terms. When He doesn't, you want me to run interfer-
ence so you can get your answers and get on with your
life."

"So?"

She shook her head. "Nice theory, but it doesn't
work like that. God does things in His time, not yours.
When you're ready to listen, He'll answer. He always
does."

Tucker thought about that while she pushed the barbecue grill back into its place by the house.

"So what you're really saying is that you *can't* help
me." He had to force the words out. Defeat dragged at
him.

"No! I *am* helping you, Tuck. I'm trying to tell you
what I've learned personally." She stood at the railing,
her eyes on the starry heavens. "I think there comes a
point in our lives when God leads us to a certain
place—a decision-making place that seems hard and
barren. Like a desert. He gives us a test, harder than

we've ever had. But the test isn't so He can figure out what we're made of. He already knows.''

"Then why?'' He moved to stand beside her, wondering what she saw in the darkness that made her skin glow with that inner radiance.

"The test is for us, to figure out where our priorities are, how willing we are to be led by Him, to get with *His* program.'' Her voice dropped to a whisper. "It isn't easy to give the controls of your life to God, and it sure isn't fast. It's more like peeling an onion. You think the problem is one thing, so you peel that away, and underneath you find something else.''

Her voice died away. All Tucker could hear was the soft croak of a few frogs.

"And then?'' he whispered, half afraid to hear her answer.

She turned to him, and he saw that her eyes were full of tears, big fat droplets that hung on her lashes for a moment, then plopped onto her cheeks.

"You keep peeling,'' she whispered. "Until you find the truth.'' She brushed the tears away, tried to smile.

Tucker turned to the sky, feeling her pain as if she were connected to him by an electrode. She'd been through it, he knew that. He could hear it in her voice, see it in her eyes. Was it his fault? Had he done that to her?

When he could stand the silence no longer, Tucker faced her squarely.

"When does the pain end, Ginny?''

She turned away, took a step toward the door. He thought she hadn't heard. But at the last moment, backlit by the kitchen, she turned to face him. Her eyes were in shadow, and he couldn't read them, but her voice conveyed everything she was feeling.

"I don't know when it ends, Tucker. I wish I did.''

Chapter Five

Several days later, Ginny pulled into the driveway, wondering exactly what she'd accomplished by attending the trade show in Denver. Nothing interested her. Nothing held her attention. Nothing made her think of new and better ways to run her business.

Instead she'd spent almost the entire time thinking of Tucker.

Move on, she ordered her weary body as she climbed out of the car. She dragged her suitcase from the trunk. Kids' voices penetrated the evening air. It sounded like they were having a ball. Lucky kids. Carefree, happy, unbound by feelings that should have died seven years ago.

"Dad? I'm home."

In the process of removing her key from the open door, Ginny stopped. That laughter was coming from her backyard! She dropped her bag and hurried through the kitchen to the deck, where she jerked to a stop. One hand flew over her mouth to stop the squeal of surprise.

"Hey, honey. Glad you're home. Did you have a good time?"

Her father lay sprawled in his lounger, his face wrinkled in a happy smile.

"What on earth is going on?" she demanded. The noise grew in volume. A squawk of protest, a shout of laughter. But Ginny couldn't see a single person.

"Two of the boys are here," her father explained. "They wanted to try the hot tub, as they call it." He picked up his paper and folded it. "They're having a great time. Tucker's watching them."

"Tucker is?" Ginny wanted to turn tail and run. Why couldn't she get away from Tucker Townsend?

Then something twigged in her brain. She studied her father thoughtfully. Everything seemed all right.

"Tucker agreed to watch two of those kids play in the water? Willingly?"

"Uh-huh. He came by the store this morning, and I got him to help me with a couple of things. Before you know it the day was gone. I ordered some pizza and invited him to have supper with me."

Ginny opened her mouth, but he hurried on, fully aware that she would have something to say about the pizza.

"The boys happened to stop by and asked if they could try the hot pool. I figured it would be okay, but Tucker said they had to lend a hand first. They mowed the grass, dug up that section of the flower bed you wanted to plant and took out the garbage for me."

"Really?" She sank down in the chair opposite his, totally flummoxed by Tucker's involvement in all this. "This is the same Tucker who wouldn't come out of his room at the Bains' for days on end?" She shook her head. "Sounds like you've had a busy time."

"I think he's lonely, honey. And lost. He just can't seem to get his act together."

"I'll go change."

It took Ginny less than five minutes to shrug out of her suit and tug on a pair of jeans and a T-shirt. She pulled a sweater on over that, slipped into her new flash-red sneakers and hurried downstairs.

We all know why you're hurrying, Virginia. She mocked herself for pretending her speed was due to anything other than Tucker's presence in the backyard. How gullible was that—especially when he'd already told her they wouldn't resume the relationship they'd shared.

Ginny shoved the thought away. He just needed time, that's all.

And she'd had a lot of practice waiting. Once the tea had steeped, Ginny filled a mug for her father, topped hers with cream and carried them outside. Then she wandered into the yard to see how the bathers were doing.

She heard Tucker's voice long before she saw him squatting at the edge of the water, skipping small stones across its surface.

"I don't know when I'll be going back, Tom. Not till I've healed, for sure."

She shifted to the left, found a grassy spot half-hidden by the trees, where she could see their faces and hear them speak.

"You look okay to me." Tom squinted, checking for some injury that would prevent Tucker's return to work.

"I feel a lot better than I did, but I've still got to take it easy. My head aches a lot." Tucker looked away from the inquisitive eyes. "There's no point going back if I'm not up to par."

Ginny thought he sounded defensive.

"True." As if he understood Tucker didn't want to say any more, Tom gave up that subject. "It must have been interesting to travel so much."

"It was. At first. I grew up in Jubilee Junction, you know. I could hardly wait to get out of here."

Ginny saw the wry smile lift one side of Tom's mouth.

"Me, too. Sometimes I think I can't wait another day for a chance to get out of here." Tom flicked a stone so it just missed Paul, who was sitting quietly in the warm water. Paul held up a fist, and Tom laughed. "This place is like all the rest, filled with a bunch of judges."

"You sure?" Tucker slanted a sideways look at him. "Maybe it's just that you haven't done anything to inspire them yet."

"Yeah. Right." Tom jutted out his chin, hunched his shoulders and scraped a finger through the sand. "What'd you do after college?" he asked Tucker.

"After college?" Tucker thought for a minute. "Went to Israel. It was my first story from a country that was troubled with war. Somebody had blown up a car, which in turn set fire to an apartment building. Fourteen people were injured."

"Badly?" Tom pretended disinterest, but the way he leaned forward to hear the answer gave him away.

Ginny smiled but stayed where she was. For the first time since he'd come back, Tucker was discussing his past. She wanted to hear what he had to say.

"It was horrible. There were these three little girls, small, you know?" Tucker stopped for a minute, sucked in a breath and continued. "They'd been playing on the sidewalk when the car blew. Their mother was burned so badly no one could identify her. In a matter of a second those kids were orphans.''

"Oh." Tom shifted uncomfortably, stood, walked away, then returned. His low voice couldn't conceal his nervousness. "Did they catch him?"

"No. But it wouldn't have mattered if they had." Tucker stood, shoved his hands into his pockets, his face grim. "How could anything make up for losing your mother, Tom?"

"Well, I don't guess that happened very often." Tom muttered the words after a long silence.

"Too many times. In my life I've seen more burn victims than I want to. It's the most painful thing imaginable." He lifted his head and looked directly at the boy. "But you must know that, right?"

"Me?" Tom bristled. "I never hurt anyone. Just burned buildings that should have been torn down. I kinda speeded up the process." He smirked, but the grin faded as Tucker kept staring at him.

"They should have! People shouldn't have to live in places like that just because they're poor." His thin shoulders jerked underneath his shirt. "Somebody should have done something. It isn't right."

"So you thought you'd make it right, fix things, by getting rid of the buildings. Is that it?"

"Yeah, man. That's exactly right." Tom leaned on his heels defiantly.

"I see." Tucker closed his eyes, pretended he was disinterested. After a moment, he asked, "Did someone build a new building on those sites, Tom? Or were the folks who used to live there left homeless?"

Tom's mouth pinched in a tight line, but he said nothing.

"Did you replace their burned photos and picture albums, their love letters? All the treasures people collect over a lifetime?'' Tucker's stern gaze dared the boy to lie.

''No.''

''I didn't think so.''

''I didn't think about where they'd live after,'' Tom admitted quietly.

''But that's pretty important, don't you think? Figuring out what happens as a result of your actions?'' He stared straight ahead, his eyes on some distant object. ''The thing you have to remember, Tom, the thing I've had to learn the hard way, is that if there's a rule, there's usually a reason.''

''Maybe.'' Tom wasn't giving an inch, his face as determined, as belligerent as ever. ''But some rules are just plain wrong no matter what the reason.'' He kicked off his sneakers and headed for the hot pool at a jog.

''Then figure out how to change the rules,'' Tucker yelled after him. ''Without breaking the law.''

Ginny waited a few moments before she headed toward Tucker. He heard her feet crunch a branch and turned with a jerk, then shifted to his original stance.

''You're very good at that.'' She stood beside him and watched the two kids splash each other. ''He'll think about what you've said.''

''I hope so. Though I haven't any right to speak the way I did. I've broken more rules than anyone. You should know that.'' He offered a lopsided smile. ''I'm glad you're back.''

By mutual consent, they sat on the grass, far enough to speak without being overheard but near enough to make sure the boys didn't court trouble.

''I've been doing some thinking of my own.'' He kicked his heel against the turf.

"Anything you want to share?" *Please, God, give me wisdom to know how to help him.*

"Maybe." It took him a while to organize his thoughts. "I read those verses you gave your dad for me." He risked a glance at her. "Ginny, I grew up believing God was there for me. To be honest, I can't *not* believe in Him."

"Go on," she whispered, to encourage him.

"It's just that lately, I can't seem to reconcile what I learned about God with what happened over there. You know? I mean, we were taught He was loving, kind, waiting to be there for us." He shook his head, his eyes flashing with anger. "Why would a God like that allow the things that go on?"

"That's an old argument, Tucker. And there are hundreds of reasons I could trot out for you."

He waited expectantly. When she didn't speak, he frowned. "But?"

"You've heard them all before." She said it bluntly, with no notion of softening her words. "I could argue pros and cons all night, explain, justify, theorize. But the truth is we will never, ever know God's reasons until we really know God."

"I know I haven't been as faithful as I should have been—"

She cut him off, lifting one hand in a peremptory gesture.

"No. Not faithful. I'm talking about a real, intimate, personal, one-on-one rapport that survives the tough times."

"Forget it." He sighed heavily. "I can't do that."

"Yes, you can. It isn't easy, it won't be fast and you certainly won't be in control, but you can know God. If you want to."

"But I've tried—"

"Have you? Or have you used Him, run to Him for comfort and help only when you couldn't manage on your own?" She laid her hand over his and squeezed. "I'm not saying that's wrong, Tucker. I'm just saying God has to be more than a big teddy bear who fixes things when we mess up. Otherwise He wouldn't be God."

Ginny rose, wandered closer to the boys. Suddenly, she had no more words. She wasn't sure of what she was trying to say.

All the way home she'd thought about Tucker's sudden return to Jubilee. It wasn't chance. Ginny was certain God had engineered events in Tucker's life for a reason. It was up to him to figure out why. It was up to her to help him.

"Hey, guys. How's the water?"

"It's great. I never knew it came out of the ground warm like this." Tom was poking and prodding the bubble where the spring erupted from the rock bed. "I wish I could see inside this stone. It's awesome."

"Yes, it is. You might try the library after school tomorrow. They've got some books on geothermal stuff. I'm sure there would be a diagram, maybe even some photos."

"The library?" Tom stared at her, a sickly look washing over his features.

"Yes. You know, the redbrick building beside the town office. Houses a lot of books." She grinned at him.

"Ha, ha." He flopped into the water, his eyes wary as they met Paul's. "Think we should check it out?"

"I guess." Paul rolled over, obviously unconcerned.

"I heard they've got a whole section of magazines on dirt bikes. I wouldn't mind seeing what's new."

"Yeah. Dirt bikes." Tom squinted at Ginny. "How am I supposed to know where to look for the—uh, others?"

"There's a woman behind a desk. She's the librarian and she knows where to find everything. She'll probably dig up more information than you could read in a year."

"Information on what?" Tucker stood behind her, his breath shifting her hair a little.

"Geothermal stuff." Tom glanced around, his eyes thoughtful. "I used to have a rock collection," he remembered. "When I was a kid."

"So did I! There's some really great ones around here." Tucker pointed to a cave in the rock face downstream. "I even found fool's gold in there once."

"Now you've done it, Tom." Ginny shook her head sadly, but she couldn't wipe the smile off her face. Here was another incidence where Tucker and the boys shared something in common.

"I did?"

"Once Tucker gets started on rocks, he never stops. He'll talk about them for the rest of the night." She sighed. "I was thinking we could go for ice cream before your curfew, but it doesn't matter." She turned to leave, fighting hard to keep the laughter inside.

"I could do with some ice cream." Paul was out of the pool in seconds. He sprinted ahead of her, one finger snagged in the belt loop of his jeans, which floated behind him in the breeze. "Be ready in a second, Ginny."

"Hey!" Tom hurled himself after Paul. "You told me you weren't taking any freebies from anybody in this town."

"Ice cream doesn't count." Paul disappeared into the

house and returned in a flash, jeans and shirt covering his thin body. Before Tom got inside the house, he'd managed to get his shoes and socks on. "I'm ready to go."

"So'm I." Tom tucked his shirt in as he spoke, then hopped from one leg to the other as he replaced his shoes. "What kind of ice cream?"

"The Dairy Shack?" Ginny nodded at their grins. Even Tucker approved. "Though I prefer frozen yogurt."

"Yogurt?" It came out in unison. Six eyes gaped at her. "No way."

"Triple chocolate almond fudge."

"Rocky Road with a twist of tiger stripe."

"Sour ball bubble gum."

Ginny stared at Tom. "Sour ball bubble gum? That's a flavor of ice cream?"

"Yeah. It's great! It has these pieces of gum that make your mouth pucker after you swallow the ice cream."

"Hm. I think I'll pass on that culinary delight." Adrian stood up, his eyes dancing. "My stomach can't take it, and neither can my waistline. Good night, boys. I appreciate your help."

"Uh, good night, Mr. Brown. And thanks a lot for the pizza. I usually get pepperoni, but your vegetable stuff was okay." Tom grinned at the older man.

Obviously the two understood each other perfectly, Ginny decided.

"Yeah, thanks," Paul echoed.

"My pleasure." Adrian disappeared inside.

"We've got forty minutes until you two have to be home. Ginny?" Tucker tilted an eyebrow.

"I'm ready. You can pile into my car."

It took several minutes for them to organize who would sit where. It amused Ginny that Tom studied every move she made, as if he didn't think she knew how to shift gears.

They chose their ice cream courtesy of Tucker, who insisted on paying, then took the last table.

"Man, this is bad." Paul licked the drips of tiger stripe off his fingers, his eyes shining.

"That's junk. Now this is excellent." Tom held up his sour ball bubble gum confection with its lime-green chunks and bright red streaks.

"You're both weird. And you have no taste. Chocolate's always been the number-one seller in this place." Tucker closed his eyes and savored the rich cocoa flavor. "Pure decadence. I haven't had ice cream like this in years."

"Didn't they have ice cream where you were?" Tom chewed on a piece of gum, forming the words around it.

"Not hardly. Some of them didn't even have refrigeration." Tucker's smile drained away. His eyes lost their glow.

"Someday, if you've got time, would you mind telling us about the places you've been?" Tom looked to Paul for confirmation. They nodded at each other. "We'd like to know what it was like."

Ginny froze in her seat, her apricot yogurt forgotten as she waited for Tucker to shut them out. She'd have to take the boys aside later, explain that he—

"Why do you want to know?"

She twisted to stare at him, surprised by the lack of emotion in his voice.

Tom frowned, his eyes on his treat.

"I'm not sure, exactly," he murmured, obviously

puzzling it through. "But when you talk about your work, you get this funny look on your face, as if you're back there and not here. I'd like to know what was so special about it."

"Me, too. I never been no place."

"Anywhere," Ginny corrected.

"You, neither?" Paul's eyebrows rose. "We sure missed out, huh?"

So much for the grammar lesson. But that wasn't important. In a flash, Ginny saw that the boys were giving Tucker a perfect opportunity to talk out the pain of his experiences. Through his words, he could lead, harness and direct their energies. They had potential, abilities. It would take skill and understanding, but she was certain that Tom, Paul and the rest of the boys could be drawn into seeing the possibilities of life.

All they needed was someone like Tucker to motivate them, show them a different path. Tucker could do that. Hadn't she seen his abilities to motivate on his newscasts?

And Tucker—wouldn't he benefit from the boys, too? He already had a rapport with Tom. They'd discussed fires, talked about a bombing. Would Tucker open up his heart even more if they asked? Wouldn't talking about the past help heal him?

"Ginny? Are you listening?" Tucker leaned forward so that his face was directly in front of hers.

"No, I am not," she told him clearly, trying to hang on to the thread of an idea that had just come to mind. "I haven't heard a thing you've said." She dumped her dripping cone into the garbage and wiped her fingers. "I have to go home now. Tomorrow is going to be busy. Everybody in the car."

Three males gave her very funny looks, but they

obeyed her summons without comment. When she
stopped in her father's driveway, the boys obediently
got on their bikes and pedaled down the street. Tucker
stood on the sidewalk, hair askew, face wrinkled in confusion.

"Did I say something wrong?"

"No." She closed and locked the car, then unlocked
the front door. "Good night, Tucker."

"Uh, yeah. Okay. Right." He stood staring as she
stepped inside. "Good night, Ginny."

She let him take precisely six steps down the sidewalk before she called.

"Tucker?"

He stopped. Looked at her. Blinked. "Yeah."

"If you want to come over tomorrow evening, we
could talk then."

"Yeah. Sure." He nodded. "What time?"

"Six-thirty? I'll make us something to eat."

"Oh. Okay. That'd be nice. Thanks."

"You're welcome." Ginny watched as he turned,
walked a few steps, then turned back. "Good night,"
she called.

"Uh-huh." He kept on walking, muttering to himself.
"If that isn't just like a woman—up one minute, off on
a tangent the next. Completely illogical."

She almost laughed. Instead Ginny closed and locked
the door, her lips curving with anticipation.

"Get your rest, Tucker. I have a hunch you're going
to need it." She climbed the stairs, grabbed a notepad
and sank down on her bed, scribbling madly as the idea
took form and shape in her mind.

At last she had it all down. Ginny read the words to
herself, delight rising inside.

"Thanks for the idea, God. It's a dilly."

Chapter Six

"Ah—could you say that again? You want me to do what?"

Tucker's mouth flopped open. Virginia Brown could not possibly have said what he thought he'd heard. Could she?

"Come on, what's the big deal, hotshot?" Her green eyes sparkled with the dare.

Ah, now she was reverting to childhood names. Two could play at that.

"The big deal, pipsqueak, is that I know zilch about organizing a boy's group. Nada. Nothing." It must be the shoes, he decided. Nobody, not even Ginny, could be clearheaded wearing shoes like that.

"What is there to know? You were a boy once. You have a college degree. You're qualified." She perched beside him on the granite boulder behind the church, the same one they'd shared years ago, the one on which they'd always decided major issues. "It doesn't have to be anything formal. Just fun."

Tucker shook his head, determined not to be sucked into her scheme.

"No, Ginny. No way. Absolutely not." Those spindly little heels must be four inches high, at least. She wasn't thinking clearly, that was it. Otherwise she'd never have suggested such a thing.

"But—"

"I will not be some kind of Boy Scout troop leader. No."

One hand smoothed her skirt over her knees while the other tried to control that mane of curls. She winked at him.

"Actually, hotshot, you already are their leader. They tag around with you when they're not in school. Yesterday you played ball with them. Today they sat beside you in church. You're already doing it."

"No, I'm not." Let her stick that bottom lip out. She could pout all she wanted. He would not be responsible for those kids. It was impossible, crazy. And he wasn't doing it.

"Hey, Ginny. Is the picnic still on?" Tom couldn't hide the eagerness any more than he could stop licking his lips. "The fried chicken and stuff?"

Tucker did a double take. "He's not talking about my picnic, is he? *My* chicken?" He was! Tucker could see the truth all over her face. "You conned me! Just for that I should refuse to come."

"Okay." She shrugged as if she couldn't care less. "Mrs. Bains told me your favorite sandwich was peanut butter and jelly. I'm sure they have lots of that in their cupboards."

Too late he remembered that the coach had taken his wife to the city for the weekend to see their grandchildren. Where the peanut butter and jelly idea had come from, he didn't know, but he was sick to death of eating it.

Sudden suspicion dawned. Ginny? She wouldn't have told them such a thing—would she? Tucker groaned. He knew full well she would, and probably had.

"I could go to the café, you know." Like he'd turn down her chicken for restaurant food. Tucker almost laughed at himself.

"You certainly could. Enjoy yourself." Ginny used his shoulder to steady herself as she balanced on those death traps she called sandals. Slowly, carefully, she walked away.

"Of course, you'll need a reservation, because Sunday brunch is always busy." Her voice sounded smug. "I have to go. Dad's waiting in the car. I'll meet you at home, guys."

"You're not coming on the picnic?" Tom stood in front of Tucker. His thin frame was slouched in his starched white shirt as if he were terribly uncomfortable. "Aw, that's no fun. We don't wanna picnic with a girl!"

"Not that Ginny's not a great girl, but we were hoping to do some fishing." Paul, the peacemaker, tried to mend the breach after one look over his shoulder at Ginny's retreating figure. His voice dropped. "Besides, she said she'd make us pie for dessert."

"You guys are a sucker for any kind of food, you know that?" Like he wasn't?

"Not any kind. I don't eat liver."

"Very discriminating of you, I'm sure." Tucker shoved to his feet, steaming apple slices under a golden crust vivid in his mind. He knew when he was beaten. "Yeah, all right. I'm coming."

They walked the few short blocks to her house, conversation rapid, interspersed with boasts from the boys about who had caught the biggest fish in his lifetime.

The little pipsqueak! She'd done it again. She'd wheedled him into a situation without even lifting a finger. But Tucker was adamant. He would *not* take on the care and leadership of these boys. They were juvenile delinquents, for heaven's sake!

He'd have to be firm, say no and stick to it. Of course, it was a good idea, one the boys would probably benefit from. But Tucker Townsend wasn't her man. Uh-uh.

The door opened two seconds after they set foot on Brown property.

"Oh. Hello, Tucker. I see you made it, after all. Come in, boys. I'm nearly finished packing the basket."

She had the nerve to wink at him!

Tucker searched for his resolve.

"Now, Tuck, if you'd just put these blueberry pies in the back of Dad's van, we can load up." She handed him two pans with tea towels covering them, her smile sickeningly sweet. "Careful. They're still warm from the oven."

Tucker didn't need to look underneath the towels. He could visualize perfectly—dark blue juice from fat berries, sweet and sticky, oozing out between flaky golden crusts. His nose twitched. Cinnamon—just a hint. His favorite spice.

"I baked some rolls this morning."

Tucker squeezed his eyes closed and wished he could staple his ears closed, too. She was doing this deliberately. That made him think. On second thought, he'd better keep his eyes and ears open for her next trick.

"Paul, you take the rolls. Nick, potato salad. Ira and John, the fishing rods are by the garage, if you could get them for me. Great. Kent, these are the dishes we'll need." She smiled. "There. I think that's it."

"Not quite." Tucker stood where he was, balancing the pies.

"Not—" She opened her eyes very wide, staring at him.

"Chicken."

"Oh, Tom's already got that," she said, laughing at him. "I'll just grab a blanket."

It was only when she skipped up the stairs that Tucker noticed Ginny had changed into jeans and a denim shirt. On anyone else, they would have looked shabby, worn. But the almost white denim clung to her long legs, accentuating their shape as if they'd been tailor-made. The shirt hid her curves, but not too much. She was gorgeous, as usual.

As she walked down the stairs, Tucker breathed a sigh of relief that the sandals were gone. Otherwise she'd break her neck. In their place she wore tattered sneakers with no heels at all.

"What about your father?"

"Mrs. Franks is treating Dad and the Armstrongs to roast beef. You know him and red meat." She flipped her glossy curls and tied a red scarf around them to hold the bulk of her hair off her face. "I'm ready."

"Go ahead, guys. We'll be there in a minute." Better to speak the truth now, get things clear. Tucker waited until the boys were out the front door. Then he faced her head-on.

"I'm not forming a boy's group, Ginny. I agree these kids are troubled. Yes, they do need help. But I am in no position to do them any good."

There. Let her deal with that.

She stood silent, watching him for a long time. Then she turned and walked to the front door.

"Okay." She shoved her keys into her pocket, her eyes steady. "Shall we go?"

Tucker went. She wouldn't give up that easily. Not Ginny. She never had. In fact, he'd been surprised she hadn't pushed harder when he'd tried to wiggle out of that promise he'd made to marry her.

It could be her pride, he supposed. All those years hanging around, waiting for a guy who never called. Maybe she really had given up on him. That hurt. Ginny Brown personified trust. If someone said they'd do something, she never doubted it. Others might scoff. Not her. She believed in people. Had she lost faith in him?

The idea bothered him no end. Tucker fastened his seat belt and slammed the door shut, his mind busy with that question.

As he sat in the passenger seat of her father's van, watching the countryside whisk past, Tucker asked himself why. What changed her mind about him? Was it the time, the reports she'd seen? Or did she not want a relationship with a man who'd killed his best friend?

"Tucker? Are you coming?"

He blinked and discovered he was the only one sitting in the van. Tucker opened his door and climbed out, trying to quash the thought that wouldn't be silenced.

Had he disappointed Ginny? He watched her organize the boys with her usual efficiency. Had he lost her trust? Pain shafted him. He hated that thought. Ginny's trust was the one thing he'd counted on.

"Come on, Tuck. Dinner's ready." She grasped his hand and tugged.

He followed like a robot, present yet somehow distanced from the laughter and the fun. He'd done it a thousand times at work—been there without really being there. Acting a part. He accepted a plate, chewed, swallowed, but tasted nothing.

No, he finally decided. Ginny was the same rock she'd always been. Nothing had changed. Her eyes still crinkled at the corners. Her mouth still flicked that quick little smile of reassurance. Ginny was still Ginny.

But the closer he looked, the more Tucker saw. Shadows clung to the green irises, never disappearing completely, even when she doubled over in laughter. Now, when no one was watching, her smile slipped away. A whisper of sadness flickered across her face. It was like the sun slipping behind a cloud. The joy was gone.

When she looked directly at him, Tucker saw the sun again. But he also caught a glimpse of something else and almost gagged at the truth. Ginny Brown struggled to retain that brash self-assurance when she was around him. Wary, careful, she suddenly seemed unsure of how he'd react.

"So do you want to, or not?"

Tucker time-warped back to their grassy knoll and focused on the question. "Want to what?"

Tom glanced at Paul, who glanced at Nick. Around the group, eyebrows were raised in tandem. Sighs of disgust were huffed out.

"Fish," they chorused in unison.

"Yeah. Maybe. After I have some pie."

Tom made a face.

"What?"

"*Some* pie? You've had two pieces already. Me and the guys were counting on sharing the last one."

"Okay." Tucker nodded. Greedy thugs! As if he'd eat two pieces of Ginny's pie and not remember. "I might fish after I've had a few minutes to digest my meal. You guys go ahead. Show us what you can do.''

"He's gonna need more than a few minutes to digest all that.''

Tucker couldn't tell exactly where the comment came from, but he figured it didn't much matter. The six of them apparently felt he'd consumed more than his fair share of Ginny's meal. After one community look, they raced to the van, grabbed rods and minnows like vultures descending on breakfast, arguing all the while. Soon they were lined up on the shore, reels whirring as they cast their lines.

"I brought a thermos of coffee, if you'd like some.'' Ginny held up a silver flask from among the objects she was repacking into the wicker basket.

Tucker stared. How did you go about asking the woman you'd promised to marry if she was upset because you'd broken your promise?

"Is something wrong?'' She frowned at him, that little flick of hesitancy evident in the way she twiddled one lock of hair. "Tucker?''

"Wrong? No. I was just thinking.'' Good fake. Now what? "I think a cup of coffee would be great. Thanks.''

"You're welcome.'' She poured, then handed it over. "You've been awfully quiet.''

"Have I? Sorry.''

"Don't apologize. It's just that I wondered if you were angry at me. I don't mean to push you about the boys, but really, Tucker, I think you and they would benefit from the time together. You've already formed a bond with Tom.''

"I have?'' Not. "What kind of bond could we have

formed? I don't even know his last name. Does he have a last name?''

"Of course he has a last name." She didn't smile. "It's Standish. Tom Standish."

"Oh."

"He's talked to you more in the past week than anyone else in the entire time he's been in town."

"That's good. I guess." He sipped the coffee. "This coffee's delicious."

"Oh, stop it!" She surged to her feet, hair flying madly across her face as her scarf fluttered to the ground.

Tucker swallowed, unable to tear his eyes away from her. Red spots of color dotted her cheeks. She was beautiful. She was also furious.

"Stop what, Ginny?" *Like you don't know. It isn't going to work, hotshot. She can see right through you.*

"Stop pretending. If you don't want to have anything to do with these kids, if you truly can't see how much they need you, then just say so."

Tucker sat where he was. He felt—embarrassed.

"What goes around comes around, Tucker. You want me to help you, but you don't want to help anyone else. Are you really so self-centered?" She flopped down and swatted the hair from her burning cheeks. "Have you changed that much?"

"Yes," he muttered, hating to say it as much as she obviously hated hearing it.

"Fine. Then I'll get someone else to help me. Marty is concerned. He'll find time for them." She twisted so her back was to him.

"Marty's almost a senior. What's he going to say to Tom that he doesn't already say at home?" *Shut up, Townsend. It's nothing to you. Butt out.*

"I don't know, Tucker. Marty's very busy, and it will only get worse when his staff starts summer vacation, but at least *he* is willing."

The arrow-straight line of her back told Tucker exactly what she thought of him in that department.

He groaned. Tucker didn't want to have this conversation, didn't want to get mixed up in anyone else's life. But most of all he didn't want Ginny to hate him.

He reached out and touched her hand. When she didn't jerk away, he threaded his fingers in hers and spoke.

"Look, Gin, I'd help them if I could. But I haven't got anything to give them. I'm empty, a shell. I don't know which end is up myself."

"Then maybe *they* could help *you*." She tossed him an arch look.

"Probably so." Might as well admit the truth, he decided.

She watched the boys for a long time, her soft hand still where it lay cradled in his. Finally she turned to face him.

Tucker blinked, surprised by tears on her cheeks.

"What's wrong with you, Tuck? What happened to make you so cavalier about another human being?"

"You know—"

"No, I don't know. I don't understand you at all. Those kids are on a spiral downhill." Her breath hiccuped as she gathered momentum. "They've done some stupid things, probably to get attention. But they're getting the wrong kind of attention. They need to know somebody cares about them, that somebody expects something from them. They need to feel part of something other than the bad boys of Jubilee Junction."

"I can't be what they need, Gin."

She stared at him. "You already are."

She got up, walked to the water and inspected the rods, her soft voice offering a comment here, a compliment there. Tucker watched, his mind tossing around her words. It was as if a battle raged in his mind.

Sooner or later I'll have to leave.

You're here now.

I have no clue how to relate to them.

Remember? Remember your own past?

Adrian Brown. That was his past. His own father had been too tied up in making a buck to spend any time teaching his son about life. Anything Tucker had learned, he'd been taught by Adrian Brown—at first because he'd peeked through the hedge and spied on him, but later because he'd been invited over for a man's time.

How Ginny had scoffed at that. But how warm, loved and valued Tucker had felt when her father had chosen to take him camping in the mountains. Just the two of them, out in the wilds.

When his father had laughed at his dreams and wouldn't help with the forms for college, Adrian Brown had spent hours helping Tucker fill in every detail.

What goes around comes around, Tucker.

"You're telling me it's payback time?" He was addressing God out loud. "What if I mess up?"

"What if you do nothing?" Ginny stood behind him, her hands on her hips. "You'll never know what you can do until you try, Tucker."

She'd been through the wringer. He heard it in the words, saw it in the way she ducked her head away from his eyes. And that was his fault.

That's when Tucker admitted that Ginny had won.

Again. It had only been a matter of time, anyway. He glared at her.

"You should come with a warning label. Small but explosive. Always succeeds."

"Tucker!" She grinned, her joy contagious. "You'll do it? Really?"

"On one condition—that you help." He glared at her. "I have no idea what we'll do with them. I'm only here for a little while. I can't see that it will matter much."

"It will matter."

He got up and stretched, accepting that from here on in, his life was going to bedlam.

"Thank you, Tucker. Thank you so much."

She wrapped her arms around him and hugged him so hard, he lost his breath. Or maybe that was because it had been so long since he'd held her, shared her confidence and joy in a future that no longer loomed dark with worry. It was as if one slim ray of brilliant white light pierced the stone around his heart and touched his soul.

For a while Tucker could keep himself busy with these boys. After that—heaven knew.

"You're welcome. I hope."

His arms crept around her waist, up her back, tangled in that mane of almost-black hair as he relished the warmth she brought into his life. He'd been in the desert for so long, starving, parched. Ginny was his oasis. Maybe it was wrong to lean on her, ask her to give when he'd let her down so badly. But Tucker wasn't sorry.

Not one bit.

"You won't regret it, Tuck. I know you won't."

After a few moments, too soon for his liking, she wiggled free, eyes dancing with jade shards of joy.

"Can I tell them?"

"No!" He glared at her, fear surging at the thought of actually doing this. "I haven't any clue how this club is going to work. I should read up on it or something before we do anything. Establish some rules."

"Why don't you let them decide how it's going to work? Get them to set the rules for belonging. Then they'll be wary about breaking them. Oh, this is great!" She whirled in pure pleasure, but her sneaker didn't follow the correct path, and she ended up tumbling onto the grass.

"This is why ballet was a wash." He plunked down beside her, affectionately patting her shoulder. "Though the tutus were kind of cute."

"Go ahead, Tucker. Call me a klutz." She rapped him on the shoulder.

"You're a klutz." For the first time that day Tucker saw the shadows leave her eyes. He lifted one hand to touch her cheek. "A very pretty klutz, though."

"Huh! That doesn't make your words any nicer." She brushed his hand away, then hugged her knees to her chest. "I just know this is the start of something really good. God has a plan for those boys. And you're part of it."

That scared him. "I wish you wouldn't say that."

"Why not?"

"I'm a washup, Gin. I've messed up. What if I do it again?" He couldn't lie, pretend it wouldn't happen. It would. He knew it.

"What if you succeed beyond your wildest dreams? What if Tucker Townsend's boy's group grows to become a worldwide phenomenon?"

He groaned, rubbed his forehead with his fingers. "You're not helping."

"All right. How about this? The first thing you need is a place to meet. I suggest a clubhouse."

"Good. A clubhouse." He fastened on that. "Where are we going to get one?"

"In our backyard." She grinned, obviously pleased with herself. "We've got that empty lot beside the river. There are tons of trees. Why don't you build a tree house?"

The words were too innocent. Suddenly Tucker figured it out. Ginny had never really accepted his no. She was so certain of him she'd planned well ahead. She probably had a detailed list somewhere.

"Ginny?" He had to stop her, make her think. *You can't talk her out of it, you know that. She's determined. She's got everything planned. She's probably even talked it over with her father.* "What will your dad say?"

"He'll tell us to go ahead. It's time it was used," she parroted, then smirked, tongue firmly in cheek.

"Aha." *What was the point of arguing with a juggernaut? Go with the flow, Townsend. She's got the faith. You can ride on her coattails.* "And the lumber for this clubhouse? I suppose you know where to find that?"

She tapped one finger on her chin, eyes brooding as they met his.

"I admit, that did give me a little pause."

"Really?" He wanted to crow with laughter. Maybe a minute's pause—certainly no longer. Not when Ginny trusted God.

"Yes. But when I was praying last night, I suddenly remembered that the church had been given some wood for the renovations on the Sunday school rooms. Apparently not all of it has been used.'' She fidgeted, thrust her legs out then pulled them back. ''Well?''

''Well, I suppose we should go take a look at it. If all else fails, we could cut down some of those trees and use that.''

''Tucker!''

Tucker laughed, deep, stomach-clenching laughs that rolled out of him when he saw the chagrin on her face.

''You wouldn't dare cut down my maples!''

''Well, we will need wood for a tree house for this club that *you* want.'' Truth to tell, he was enjoying the idea now that he'd gotten used to it. Maybe for a while he could let the world go and be a boy again.

''But I planted those when I was ten. It was my science project. Don't you remember?''

She looked so forlorn, Tucker relented, but not completely.

''As if I could forget. You nearly cut my leg off wielding that spade around. As it was I took twelve stitches for those trees.'' He winced at the memory.

''Well!'' She glared at him. ''You tried to make me put them in neat little rows. As if you make a woods with neat little rows of trees! That's an orchard, not a woods.'' She huffed her indignation. ''Anyway, I don't suppose maple is particularly good for a tree house.''

''Who's building a tree house?'' Tom stood in front of them, a stringer with fish dangling from his hand.

''We are,'' Ginny announced, jumping to her feet.

''You and Tucker are building a tree house? Oh.'' Tom stared at the fish, then lifted his eyes to Tucker's, a question lurking in the depths. ''Doesn't she like it at home?''

"Cute. Very cute." Tucker faked a smile. *Can't quite say the words, can you, Townsend? Scared of six young boys?*

Yes! his mind screamed. *Scared stiff.*

"*We're* building it, all of us. Hey! Paul, Nick, everyone, come here!" Ginny danced from one foot to the other as if the grass scorched her toes. Her hair bounced, bobbing and shimmering with a life all its own.

Once more Tucker was reminded of the past, of an evening seven years ago when her excitement had overcome all inhibition and she danced across the deck in the same way.

You promise, Tuck? You absolutely, positively promise? You won't break your word and forget me?

"Tucker, tell them why we want to build a tree house."

Tucker came to the present with a thunk. He cleared his throat, his mouth suddenly dry and sticky at the expectation revealed on seven faces. The words would not come. He tried to swallow and couldn't.

"Tucker has this great idea. He wondered if you guys wanted to form a club. A boy's club. He was thinking maybe a tree house could be your clubhouse. You could meet there every week, do all sorts of fun things over the summer." Ginny glanced from the boys to Tucker, waiting, watching.

"A boy's club? Like us six and you?" Tom stared at Tucker. "Doing stuff together?"

Nod, Townsend. Make some response. Don't just stand there.

"Yes. Us and anyone else who wanted to join." Tucker nodded, his neck stiff. *What on earth was he doing?*

"We'd have to have rules. Not just anybody can walk in and be a member of our club." Tom met Tucker's stare and blushed, his carrot head vying with his face for most color. "I guess rules do have a place," he mumbled.

Tucker sat down. He had to. His knees would no longer support the weight of his body.

"What kind of rules?" He cleared his throat. "Sorry. Guess I'm allergic or something. My voice feels funny."

Ginny sat beside him and slipped her hand into his surreptitiously so no one could see. Her smile encouraged him.

Ginny had faith. If she believed God could make some good out of this club thing, he'd hang on to that. For now.

"Well, I dunno." Tom set his fish carefully in the bag he'd brought, then flopped down across from them. "We don't want nobody in our group that doesn't have the same rules we do."

"Yeah, like curfews and stuff."

The others nodded.

"No smoking," Nick suggested.

Tucker stared. "Do any of you smoke?" he asked.

They shook their heads.

"Then—" Tucker stopped, his eyes on Tom's down-cast head. Something clicked. Fire. Smoking. Probation. "Good. Smoking's bad for everybody. Rule number one. No smoking. Next?"

They argued, debated and finally settled on the rest of the rules until the boys had hammered out nine ab-solutes.

"And no girls. That's number ten."

Tucker glanced at Ginny, wondering how she'd take that.

"Except for Ginny," Paul inserted. "She's our special guest. She can come any time we invite her. Especially if she brings food.'' He grinned.

The others nodded.

Ginny accepted their ruling with grumbled good grace.

''I feel compelled to tell you that at some point in the future girls are going to become very important to you.'' Tucker almost laughed at the looks on their faces.

''As if!''

''It's true. Soon you'll be wanting to date, to bring them to our meetings, to show them the clubhouse.'' Tucker chuckled at their skepticism, his eyes meeting Ginny's fun-filled ones.

''Never!'' The vote was unanimous.

''Just remember what I said.''

Fish forgotten, they began scratching out blueprints in the sand, growing more excited with every line.

''You'd better rethink it, guys.'' He should take his own advice. ''It's a clubhouse. In a tree. There won't be all that much room.'' Tucker shook his head at the elaborate plans.

''Well, how are we going to do stuff if we don't have room?'' They sat back, waiting for an answer.

''What kind of stuff?'' He should have asked first and volunteered later. A little hesitation was a good thing.

''Projects and stuff. You know.''

That was the trouble. He didn't know. He had no clue what he was doing here, and in about thirty seconds they were going to know it.

''He's right. The clubhouse should be for official meetings. Brainstorming. That kind of thing.'' Tom stared at the sketches, his body tilted slightly forward.

"But I might know someplace we could go, you know, to build stuff. Or whatever."

"Yeah? Where?" New respect filtered through the others as they waited for his answer.

"My dad—my foster dad. He has some basement rooms at the paper. He might let us use them." Tom looked straight at Tucker. "As long as we had someone responsible with us."

Responsible? Him? Prickles feathered up and down Tucker's arm. He tried to swallow the lump of fear, but his mouth was so dry, words wouldn't come. He didn't even know what he wanted to say! All he felt was a deep, cloying apprehension.

"That's a good idea, Tom. I'm sure Tucker won't mind asking Marty tomorrow."

He heaved a sigh of relief as Ginny drew their attention away from him. But what was he going to do when she wasn't there?

"Right now I think we'd better clean up. I've got to head home. Dad'll be wondering what happened." She stood and began shaking out the blanket she'd sat on. "This was a good day, guys. A very good day."

Was it? Tucker wasn't so sure.

But he helped her clean up. They packed the van and he rode back to her house without blurting out his fears. It was only when he sat alone in his room at the Bains' that the enormity of what he'd agreed to sunk in.

Okay, maybe running back to Ginny and Jubilee Junction wasn't so smart after all.

Chapter Seven

"Marty? Hi. How are you?"

"I'm okay, Tucker. How're you doing? You look a little less battered than the last time I saw you. Feeling all right?" The older man scrutinized him thoroughly, but there was kindness in the depths of his eyes.

"Well, I was." Tucker shook his head. "Now I think I might have had a touch too much sun on Sunday. Either that or Ginny Brown conned me big time." Tucker took the proffered seat and leaned back, watching Marty's grin appear.

"Ginny, huh? Well, she's always gone after what she wants. What's the problem?" Marty shuffled a stack of papers off his chair and onto the floor before he flopped down and tilted back, eyes curious. "You get another assignment or something?"

"Sort of." He told him about the boy's club. "The thing is, Tom sort of volunteered some space you had in the basement for a kind of workroom."

"He did, huh? Good for Tom. I'm glad he's taking

an interest in something.'' Marty's lined face brightened. ''Workroom for what?''

Now for the hard part. Tucker winced as he heard himself say it.

''I haven't got a clue.''

''Huh?'' Marty stared.

''I mean it. I have no idea what to do with that bunch. Boy's club sounds good in theory, but practically, what do you do with a bunch of kids who've been in trouble with the law?''

''Keep 'em very busy.'' The newspaper editor grinned. ''I mean it, Tuck. They need something to care about, something they can get involved in.''

''That's where I was hoping you'd come in. Got any ideas?'' Tucker waited, his breath stuck somewhere in his chest, while Marty considered the question.

''As a matter of fact I do.'' The editor dug around in a corner for several minutes before unearthing a battered and bashed brown box. ''See this?''

''You want them to build boxes?'' Oh, this was going to be some club!

''Nope.'' He dropped the contents on his desk. ''Here. You take a look.''

Tucker unfolded the white paper, chagrin slowly giving way to delight as he saw the contents. ''You're kidding!''

''I've been wanting to get that thing done for ten years. Just never got around to it. Kind of hoped Tom and I might find some common ground with it.'' He scratched his chin. ''I used to have quite a collection, years ago.''

''And the pieces are all here?'' Tucker peered into the box.

''Every one. It's painstaking work, though, Tuck.

And touchy." He fingered the balsa wood with the tip of his little finger.

"I know. But a remote-control airplane—" Tucker couldn't believe it. "It's perfect."

"It's something." Marty tipped his chair again, eyebrows meeting in a frown of concentration. "But it's just *one* thing. We'll have to do more than that with this bunch."

Tucker set the plans for the airplane inside the box and closed it. Marty was right. He'd been so relieved he hadn't thought it out. "Like what?"

"Well, I think they'll appreciate their club and this plane more if they have to work for it. There's glue to buy, fabric for the wings. And a motor. That's going to be the biggest expense." He scribbled a figure on his yellow pad and held the pad up so Tucker could read what he had written.

"That much?"

Marty nodded. "Easy."

"You think they should earn the money." Tucker figured that wasn't likely to go over well. These kids weren't used to earning anything, as evidenced by their court records. If they wanted something, they just took it.

"They'll take more pride in their achievements if we don't just hand it to them." A flicker of a smile twitched. "I've got an idea about that, too, if you want to hear it."

"Why d'you think I'm here, Marty?" Tucker grinned. "Ginny's plans notwithstanding, I'm not aiming to take on six ruffians by myself. I need a partner."

"Notwithstanding? You talk like a lawyer." Marty

grinned. "I'd like to be your partner in this, Tuck. I'd really like that." They shook on it. "Now, tell me what you think of this?"

They spent two hours hashing out the details, and by the time the big clock chimed noon across the town square, Tucker was more than pleased with their plan.

"We could hold the first meeting tomorrow night. I had a look at those trees behind Ginny's, and I don't think putting up a tree house is going to be hard." Tucker stretched. "I better get going. Thanks, Marty. It's obvious you're the brains behind this operation."

Marty turned from his stance at the window, his mouth quirked at one corner as he squinted at Tucker.

"Nice compliment, but I don't think so, son. The brains of this plan is walking out the door of her father's store right now, and you know it. Seems like Ginny just can't help helping people."

Tucker joined him at the window, finding Ginny's quick, lithe form without any difficulty.

"Yeah. She's so good at *helping,* you and I are doing the work," he grumbled.

"Oh, she'll be there, son. Won't be able to help herself. She's got her finger in more pies than a baker." Marty chuckled, letting the blind fall into place.

Tucker kept watching, narrowing his eyes to peer through the slats as he watched her. "She doesn't go home for lunch?"

"Today's Monday, isn't it?"

"Uh-huh."

"Then she's heading for Mrs. Wheeler's house. Ethel doesn't eat properly now that Ed's gone. Ginny goes over for lunch on Mondays, and the old girl cooks up a storm that lasts the rest of the week."

"She eats the same thing for a whole week?" Tucker made a face but never moved his eyes off Ginny.

She had on some kind of floppy shoes today. The brightly striped soles slapped against her heels as she trotted to the front door of a big redbrick house.

"No. Ethel and Ginny make TV dinners out of the leftovers and freeze them. They been rotating the menu for ages so that now Ethel's got a whole freezer full of decent food. Every so often she invites everybody in her Sunday school class over, and we have a potluck from her freezer."

Tucker barely heard. His eyes were stuck on Ginny as she wrapped the elderly woman in a hug. He was sorry when they disappeared inside and the door closed.

"Sounds like a good idea to me."

"Yeah, it's pretty effective. She helps out a lot of the seniors." Marty stopped speaking long enough to deal with a few questions from his assistant, then answered the phone. "I'm sorry, Tuck, but I've got to go down and deal with this. The weekly comes out Wednesday, and I can't afford to have the printer on the fritz."

"Don't apologize. You're busy, Marty, and I'm holding you up. I'll get out of your way." Tucker moved to the door, pulled it open as he spoke. "I don't know how I can ever thank you for pitching in like this."

"I do." There was a funny little gleam in Marty's eye.

"Name it." Tucker waited, flinching when that unusual look got much brighter.

"I've got two and a half columns on the second page that need filling."

"Marty, I don't—"

"Fill it however you like. Talk about your work over

there, what it's like to come home, I don't care. Just
get it to me by tomorrow morning.''

"But I—"

"Boss, I think you'd better come. Now!" A harried
woman cast one glance at Tucker, as if to tell him to
leave, before focusing all her attention on Marty.

"I've got to go, Tuck. You get the boys set for tomorrow night. We'll meet in back of Ginny's. And get
me that column.''

He scurried away, belting out questions so fast
Tucker's head spun.

Tucker wasted ten minutes staring after him. How in
the world had that happened? One minute they were
hashing out a boy's program, the next he was writing
columns? Apparently Ginny Brown wasn't the only one
who could conscript people to do what she wanted.

He finally roused himself enough to cross the room,
walk down the worn oak stairs and let himself out the
front door of the paper.

"Hi, Tucker." Ginny looped her arm through his,
matching him step for step.

"Ginny. What are you doing here?" He cast a quick
glance over his shoulder at the Wheeler house.

"Oh, my lunch date had an unexpected male friend
come to call. Things looked promising for the two of
them, so I butted out." She grinned at him. "And
you?"

He muttered something about Marty.

"He's sure got lots of ideas about kids. He and his
wife wanted children, you know, but it just never
worked out." Her shoes smacked an even rhythm to her
words. She grinned at him. "Wanna share lunch?"

"Depends." A guy had to be careful with Ginny.

"On what?"

"On what you'll try to feed me. Every time you offer me food, I end up taking on more work."

She giggled, joy bursting out of her. "Don't be silly! I'm not like that at all."

It felt good to have her arm in his, to tease her and see her eyes sparkle. It was as if he'd never left.

"All the same, I think I'd better buy this time."

"Really?" She stopped short, eyes round, lips glistening as she licked them in anticipation. "I know exactly what I want."

"So do I." Tucker grinned at her frown. "Know exactly what you want, I mean. Zanyk's chicken salad on brown, toasted, and a triple-thick milk shake," he recited. "With a dill pickle," he added, before she could.

Suddenly his courage deserted him. What if she'd changed so much she didn't like the same things anymore?

Ginny's laugh chased away the fears.

"You remembered!" One hand patted her hip where the white lawn skirt floated upward in a gust of wind. She frowned as she considered her options.

"I shouldn't, you know."

"You shouldn't?" He could hardly believe it. "Why shouldn't you?"

"That mayo alone adds five pounds after you eat it. And a milk shake—well, let's just say fat is *not* our friend." Then she shrugged, lifted her hands and grinned. "But I'm going to eat it anyway, and enjoy every bit. I'll just have to walk more this afternoon."

He led the way to Zanyk's Grill. "What's this afternoon?"

"This afternoon I have to scope out a site. The Harders are building a new house, and they've hired me to design it." Her chin lifted proudly as she described the property. "I want to take a second look at what the lot looks like in relation to the sun."

"The sun was always a big part of your life, wasn't it?" Tucker gave the order, than sat beside her on a bar stool. "You're like those flowers, I forget the name. They only open when the sun shines on them."

She wiggled to get comfortable. Tucker waited for her to pick up the threads of their conversation.

"The sun is very important to me," she admitted. "I get cranky if it's gone for a few days. I don't know how anyone could live in Seattle with all that rain." Ginny looked around. "Just imagine this place without a few sunbeams to lighten it up."

Tucker didn't need to look. He didn't think Zanyk's had changed one whit in seven years. And even with the sun, it seemed as dark and gloomy as ever. Sort of like his future.

"Hey, Gin, can we make this a carryout? I'd like to scope out this property with you." He endured the funny look she gave him. "I mean it. We could even sit in that sun you like so much."

"A picnic? Yes. Good idea. On one condition."

Uh-oh. He wasn't fond of Ginny's conditions. They always got him into trouble.

"I'm scared to ask."

"Smart man." She grinned. "I get to ride on the back of your bike."

He thought it over, then nodded. What could happen? "Okay."

"You mean it?" In her exuberance, she hugged him. "Oh, Tucker, I lo—" Her voice choked and died, her eyes cloudy, shimmering with unshed tears.

Slowly her arms dropped from his shoulders.

"I'm sorry," she whispered. "I didn't mean—" She

cleared her throat, grabbed her purse and stood. "I'll wait outside. I don't think it should be much longer."

"Ginny, it's—" He gulped down the words he'd been going to say. It wasn't all right. Not at all. He'd told her he didn't want to marry her, that he couldn't love her. Why add fuel to the fire, make it worse by repeating it all, rehashing it in a public place?

He let her go, shame welling up at her hurried departure. What a fiasco. And it was all his fault.

Several of the customers glanced up when she rushed past them without answering their calls, but no one said anything. They simply stared at Tucker with pity in their eyes.

By the time he walked outside with their lunch, Tucker had determined his next course of action. He was going to ignore her slip, pretend nothing had changed, just like he ignored the pain deep inside his soul. What else was there to do?

He found her sitting on a brilliant blue bench in front of the craft store two doors over. She got up as soon as she saw him, but her steps weren't the bouncy, buoyant ones he'd seen earlier.

"I think they gave us twice what we ordered," he joked, storing the box on the holder at the back of his bike. "Hopefully we won't blow a tire on the way back—from all the extra weight," he explained when he caught her puzzled stare.

"Ah." That was all she said as she stood, patiently waiting for him to tell her where and how to sit before handing her a helmet that matched his own.

"Okay, I think we're ready. I'll get on first." He swung his leg over and flopped on the seat, edging forward to give her as much room as possible.

That's when he caught sight of her shoes.

"Uh, Gin, I'm not sure what you're wearing is appropriate—" He stopped short at the glower in her eyes.

"You're not backing out, Tucker. Not this time. You promised I could ride on this bike, and I'm holding you to your promise this time." Her eyes glittered with an inner fury that dared him to deny her.

Which he had no intention of doing, but maybe now wasn't the time to explain. Tucker sighed. Coming back was getting a lot more complicated than he'd imagined. Everything seemed to hark back to the past, to that stupid promise. He hated watching the flicker of hurt wash over her face, hated knowing he'd put it there, but—

Ah, therein lay the problem. That little *but* hid myriad minefields, places he'd rather not explore. If that made him a coward, he'd have to learn to live with it. Somehow.

"Well?" She stood beside him, hands on her hips, waiting.

There was no avoiding this.

"Climb on. Make sure your skirt is tucked under you and your feet stay clear of mine. Most of all, make sure you don't lose those—shoes. Okay?"

"Yes!" She tossed her head, and her shiny hair bounced off her shoulders, swooped, then settled around her cheeks as she concentrated on straddling the leather seat. "Like this?"

He glanced back. She sat gingerly, as if afraid the bike would take off and eject her at any minute. Her hands fluttered nervously. She tucked her skirt more firmly around her long legs.

"Yeah, fine," Tucker muttered over the lump in his throat.

She looked like a kid who'd just been given a very special treat. Her green eyes glowed emerald in her pale heart-shaped face. Her small, compact body tilted slightly forward, ready, expectant.

"You're sure this is right?" She licked her lips. "I don't want to fall off halfway down the road."

"You won't fall off." Tucker gunned the engine once. "You can either hang on to me or to that metal bar behind your seat."

He felt her lean backward and turned to check. She was stretched to the max, trying to reach the support, her fingers barely able to close around the cold, hard metal.

"Uh, I don't think that's going to work. You'll break your back before we go half a mile. You'd better hold on to me." He waited a minute until she'd rearranged herself. "Ready?"

"Yes." A puff of warm air caught him on the neck as her fingers gripped his waist. "I'm ready."

Tucker kicked the bike into gear, wondering if he was.

It was glorious!

The wind tore at her hair, dragging it off her face so the sun could beat down and warm her. The engine throbbed beneath her, leashed power just waiting to be set free. In a kaleidoscope of impressionist paintings, the countryside whirled past, mere daubs of color.

Freedom.

Absolute freedom.

This had to be what it felt like. No wonder he loved this bike. Her dad, the store, Tucker, everything faded into the background as Ginny relished the joy of the ride.

"Okay?" Tucker called over his shoulder.

She leaned forward so her lips were near his ear.

"Perfect," she told him, and meant it.

This was why he disappeared so many nights when the boys had gone home and her father was in bed. To ride his bike and clear away the cobwebs life brought.

A thousand different fragrances assaulted her nostrils, daring her to identify them. Grass—freshly mown. Lilacs. Sweet clover. His aftershave.

It felt good to rest on him, to let herself relax, allow her body to bend with the curves in the road. Tucker was here, solid, trustworthy. He would handle things. For now, she could depend on him.

As the trees, rolling hills and scattered acreages flew past she let herself daydream, allowed just this once those fantasies from the past to live again. They were a couple, in love, secure in the world they'd built together. Nothing could keep them apart.

"Is this the place?"

Ginny opened her eyes. Reality flooded back, and with it embarrassment. She sat pasted against him, her hands tight around his middle, her face on his shoulder. Gingerly she eased away.

"Yes, this is it. Go a little farther." She sat quietly as he steered up the road, really more of a track, waiting until they crested the hill. "Stop here. Please."

"Yes, ma'am." He tossed her a grin at the order but obediently rolled the bike to a halt and turned off the motor.

Before he could see the embarrassed red covering her face or see things in her eyes she'd rather keep secret, Ginny hopped off the bike and walked to the spot her customers had chosen more than three years ago.

"Perfect," she whispered.

"It's a lovely area. They were lucky to be able to buy this."

"It wasn't luck." She sat on the grass and waited while Tucker set the box of lunch beside her.

"Really?" He accepted his milk shake, flopped down across from her as he tasted it. "What, then?"

Ginny handed him his lunch, unwrapped her own and took a bite, chewing thoughtfully on the diced celery and savory chicken before she spoke.

"Shared dreams, sacrifices, mutual plans for their future. Scrimping and saving to keep up the payments on this place." She sipped her shake, recalling what little she knew of the couple.

"Yvonne's worked more overtime, more holidays, more nights than any other nurse I know. Wayne deliberately takes all the long-haul routes he can get because they pay more. They started out with nothing, but now they've got a solid base for the future."

Out of the corner of her eye she watched Tucker's face as he assessed what she was saying.

"Wayne wants to start a cattle operation someday, so they needed extra land. Yvonne wants to raise her kids in the country, just as she was. They've got their future all mapped out."

"And you're going to do the house?" He grinned at her. "Have you got something in mind?"

"Of course." Ginny frowned. Had he really changed so much he couldn't imagine what this stretch of land could become?

Had that part of him died, too?

"Can't you see it? The kitchen's over there, to catch the morning sun. There's a breakfast nook and a larger eating area that faces south, with patio doors opening onto a big deck."

It was clear that, though Tucker looked, he didn't see what she did.

"No dining room?"

She'd give him a point for trying.

"No dining room. They don't want formal, they want family. Comfort but also efficiency."

"Ah." He looked dubious.

"That doesn't mean it's going to be ugly, Tucker. I think they'll be very happy with their new home when it's finished." She couldn't resist telling him the rest.

"A family room sits opposite the kitchen so they can still have those big family dinners without sending everyone to a different room. Wayne's study will be in front, across from Yvonne's workroom, which will include the laundry. The bedrooms are—" She stopped, only then noting his glazed expression. "You're not interested, are you?"

"Interested, yes. But I guess I'm not good at visualizing. A picture would help." He used a napkin to wipe the last bit of chicken salad from his finger. "It's funny, but I never thought of you as particularly talented at seeing what isn't there, either."

"You might be surprised." Ginny crunched on her pickle, deliberately avoiding the words that longed to tumble out. She knew he didn't want to go backward, knew he hated dragging up the past. But for her, past and future ran together, one inexplicably entwined with the other.

"When you see the future, Gin, what do you see?"

The whisper-soft question shocked her. What was he really asking? Could it be that he sometimes thought about the promise he'd made, wondered if she did?

Did he want to know her heart's desire? Did he care?

She sipped her drink, her mind filling with possibilities.

"Gin? What do you see when you look into the future?"

You. She didn't say it.

Instead Ginny stared at Tucker, watched his eyes darken with worry. "I'm not sure," she finally admitted.

"Is it because of me? Do you think that if I stay here long enough I'll change my mind?" The voice was soft, but the words were harsh.

She refused to look at him, knowing that was exactly what she thought, hoped, prayed, ever since he walked into town. She'd tried to stifle her feelings, pretend they weren't there, even ignore them.

And now she was totally confused.

"I—"

"It can't happen, Virginia. I won't let it. My future isn't here, if it ever was, and I'm beginning to doubt even that."

He sprawled on the grass, his eyes searching the heavens, though Ginny was almost certain he didn't know what he sought.

"I would never presume to tell you that you should stay." She put the rest of her sandwich into the bag, hunger completely gone.

"You asked me what I see in my future, Tucker. The answer is, I don't look that far any more. Living today, that's all I can handle. I get up in the morning, pray that God will give me enough strength to handle whatever comes up, and I take the next step. Right now that's all I can manage."

"You can see houses not yet built, but you can't see your own future?" He smiled lopsidedly. "That doesn't sound like the Ginny I knew."

A tear wiggled out of the corner of her eye and trickled down her cheek. Ginny dashed it away, angry with herself for letting him see her emotion.

"Perhaps that's at the root of everything." She glared at him. "I'm not the Ginny you knew, Tucker. I'm older, maybe wiser. Nothing is black and white anymore in my life. I can't say, 'I'm going to go here, or I'll do that,' because the truth is I probably won't."

"And that's okay with you?" He sat up as if that would give him a better take on her expression.

"It doesn't matter if it's okay with me or not."

"It doesn't?"

She shook her head. "I'm not the one in control. God is. He knows what I want to happen. He knows the deepest secrets of my heart. And He wants to give me what's best. So I follow His lead. So far that's meant staying in Jubilee Junction and working with my dad."

"But it sounds so—fatalistic!"

"Oh, no! It's not fatalistic at all. It's faith."

"I don't get it." He raked a hand through his hair, frustration burning in his eyes.

"When I gave my life to God, I handed over the reins and promised He'd be Lord. That means He's the boss. I do what He wants, not the other way around." Even as she said the words, Ginny wondered if Tucker realized how difficult that was sometimes.

"So you just sit around and wait for some miracle to happen?"

"Is that what you think? That I've been sitting around these past seven years?" She burst out laughing at the dubious look on his face. "I haven't got time to sit around, Tucker. I've got a business to run, houses to build, a degree to finish."

"But that's what I meant when I asked about your future."

"Did you?" She fiddled with her skirt, avoiding his eyes. "I thought you were asking about whether I expected to marry, have a family, travel."

"In a way, that, too." He pulled up a blade of grass and stuck it between his teeth. "So you don't want those things?"

"I didn't say that."

Where was this going? What exactly was he asking? If she still loved him?

"Then what *are* you saying? Speak plain English, Gin. Stop dancing around and lay it out so I can understand!"

She twisted her body so her eyes were only inches from his. His chocolate-scented breath feathered over her face.

"I'm not dancing around anything." She held his gaze while searching desperately to put her feelings into words. "I can't look that far ahead, Tucker, because I don't know if that's what God has in store for me. If He does, fine. There's nothing I'd like better than to be a wife and mother."

His eyes met hers, fear swirling in their depths. He leaned back a fraction, trying to escape her stare.

"And if not?"

The whispered words pierced her to the quick, but Ginny managed to retain her composure.

"If not, then God will give me the strength and grace to pursue something else, something far more wonderful that He has in store."

"I hate that!" He pushed himself away from her and jumped to his feet, pacing a narrow track across the hilltop. "I just hate it." His hands were clenched at his sides. His teeth barely allowed the whispered words to be heard.

"Why?" Ginny stayed where she was, sensing he needed the space.

"Because it renders you so helpless, as if you're at the mercy of some unknown fate." He glared at her, the anger barely suppressed.

Ginny smiled. She knew exactly how he felt. She'd fought her way through this often enough before she'd finally accepted the truth.

"I am at the mercy of the unknown," she murmured, staring at the azure sky with a faint smile. "But not at the mercy of fate. Never that."

"God, you mean." It wasn't a question.

"That's exactly Who I mean."

"And you think it's okay that God would take away the one dream you talked about for as long as I've known you?" He glared at her.

"Tucker, it's not only okay with me, it's the only way I want it."

"Ginny, that's ridiculous."

She stood, allowed the wind to blow her hair, to press her cotton skirt against her legs. Somehow it was freeing, as if the breeze that buffeted her carried away all the doubts and fears that tried to sneak up on her during the calm.

"No, it's not ridiculous." She touched him on the arm, indicating the land on which they stood, the wildflowers nodding across the meadow, the wooded area that sheltered a creek.

"He's God, Tucker. *God.* He has more power, more brains, more intelligence than I could possibly imagine. He created me. How could I ever tell Him what He should be doing? If He's truly *my* Lord, then it's unthinkable that I, the servant, would give Him orders or try to get my own way."

She stared at the land she'd chosen for the building site, awestruck once more as she contemplated the mighty hands that had created such beauty.

"He's Almighty God, Tucker," she whispered. "I daren't challenge His decisions."

She closed her eyes and listened as the wind whispered through the dried grass surrounding them, felt the soft, gentle caress across her face and knew that she was right.

God was in control.

"I guess we'd better head back. If you're finished."

"Yes, I'm finished." Ginny opened her eyes and smiled at him, misty-eyed. "We can go anytime."

They climbed on the bike, him in front, her behind, holding on to his middle. On the open highway, Ginny closed her eyes, ready to recapture the sense of awe and wonder she'd felt up there.

Instead her heart clicked into overdrive and presented her with the knowledge she'd been so carefully avoiding.

I love him. It hasn't died or gone away or decreased. I love him in spite of his doubts, his broken promise, his refusal to love me back.

Once more she closed her eyes, but this time when she rested her head on Tucker's back, Ginny wasn't daydreaming. This time she prayed for the man who needed her only as a means to escape his past.

Oh, please, God, show me what to do now.

Chapter Eight

"Okay, guys, that's it for tonight."

"Hey, we haven't got half of the stuff done!" Tom glowered at Marty and Tucker, his stance deliberately belligerent.

"No, we haven't. But what we do have is a very good basic framework to begin our club and a semifinished clubhouse." Tucker met the glare with a warning look. "We also have a curfew coming up, and if that's broken, this club is history."

"Stupid curfews!" Kent kicked a clod of dirt six feet into the air.

"It's life, kid. Get used to its rules. Only at my age, we call them deadlines." Marty grinned, ruffled his hair and made a notation on the pad he carried. "If you guys can find odd jobs folks around town want done, that would help raise some funds for our plane. We can't fly it without a motor."

"I saw a shaggy ol' lawn by my house. I could ask about mowing it."

"Yeah, and there's that woman with all those flower beds by me. Somebody's gotta dig 'em for her."

The boys all joined in, and the list of things grew exponentially.

"You've got the general idea. See you on Friday." Tucker waved them off and turned to Marty. "You go ahead. I want to get some of this mess cleaned up. If Ginny's dad goes for a walk, he'll kill himself on our odds and ends."

"Thanks, man. By the way, how's the column coming?" Marty blinked at him innocently, pretending they were in total agreement on the subject.

"It's not. One write-up. That's all I agreed to do."

"Tucker, your first column was fantastic! Just wait till people get a chance to read it tomorrow, and you'll see how great you are at this stuff."

Great. Yeah, right. He'd prattled on about the landscape in Africa, the lush forests and the sparse poverty. He'd stayed away from discussing his job. He wasn't going there. No way!

"I'm serious. The way you describe things makes them personal, close. People like that. They feel like they can see the world through your eyes." He clapped a hand on Tucker's shoulder. "It's a gift, man."

"Yeah, a gift." Now that was funny.

"That fund-raising group Ginny's leading will want to know more. You know that, don't you? You've only whetted their appetite."

Tough. Tucker wished he'd never allowed himself to be conned into it in the first place.

"You could always discuss somewhere else," Marty suggested. "You've traveled all over the place."

Tucker nodded. "I guess."

But Africa was *his* beat, his favorite place in all the

world. And now it had been ruined, tarnished, stained by something that should never have happened.

"I don't think I can write any more, Marty. I've got enough on my plate as it is." He kept his voice low, avoided the other man's eyes and the pity he knew he'd find there.

"It's up to you, of course. But I'd really appreciate it. So would the rest of Jubilee Junction." Marty waved a hand and walked across the street to his car. Seconds later he was gone, and Tucker was alone.

He forced himself to ignore the protest of muscles not fully healed by concentrating on clearing the branches into a huge pile, out of sight of the Browns' home.

"It's a good start." Adrian Brown stood behind him, his eyes on the freshly begun tree house. "You've got your work cut out for you with those boys."

Tucker grabbed one of the folded lawn chairs he'd stood against a stump and opened it up.

"Here, have a seat."

"Thanks." Adrian sank into it with relief, unable to hide the strain around his mouth.

"You're sure you want to be out here?" Tucker wrestled the last of the branches onto the heap, then sank onto the grass, feeling just as tired as Adrian Brown looked.

"I'm sure. I need some fresh air."

Something in the words sent Tucker's head jerking up to inspect the older man.

"Why?"

"I've got myself a little problem." Ginny's father tilted his head against the chair, slouching, eyes closed, breathing slowly, deliberately.

"You know what's wrong with you." It was the only

explanation. Tucker's fingers wrapped around themselves a little tighter, but he said no more, waiting.

"I don't, but the doctors think they might." He straightened, opened his eyes and peered at Tucker in a Ginny-like glare that was uncanny. "At the appointment today one of them tried to prepare me for the possibility of stomach cancer. If they're right, my daughter's going to need every friend she has."

Adrian wanted to know if Tucker would be around when Ginny's grief required a shoulder to lean on. But how could Tucker give his word to a man who was facing the biggest challenge of his life when Tucker knew he couldn't keep his promise?

"Does Ginny know?"

Adrian's stare did not abate in spite of Tucker's silence. When he finally spoke, his words shocked Tucker beyond belief.

"No. And she won't. Not until they've diagnosed it for certain. Not until I can't keep from telling her. Do you understand?" Adrian's tortured eyes begged him to grasp his meaning.

"Yes." Wanting to spare a loved one? Yeah, Tucker knew about that. He understood the need to protect her from pain. Wasn't that what he'd told himself he was doing for seven years?

The silence of the evening closed in around them. Birds twittered more softly as they nested for the night. Children's voices quieted, then disappeared as parents shuffled them off to bed. At last there was only the soft whisper of wind through the leaves, the periodic hum of a car engine passing out front, the gurgle of the water running down the riverbed.

"Tell me," Adrian murmured, closing his eyes once

more. "Tell me about your time over there, Tucker. All of it."

Tucker cringed, forcibly containing the words. No! He didn't want to say it, think about it, relive it all over again. Weren't the nightmares enough?

"Please tell me, Tucker. Help me forget my pain for a while."

That soft, plaintive request was his undoing. Tucker inhaled, filling his lungs with fresh, new air as he let out the foulness of the past.

"It was summer over there, hot, humid, unbelievably sticky. Tensions were so high you could cut them with a knife. There'd been a riot. Another one."

Ginny heard the murmur of voices from her position on the back porch. She studied the gloomy dusk for her father's familiar stooped figure, but she couldn't see him.

Curious, she stepped off the deck and walked the length of the backyard, ears pricked as words and phrases floated toward her on the night air.

"...bombs. I close my eyes and I can still smell the stench of it. Burning rubber, petrol. And the voices. Oh, my Lord, the voices. They screamed with terror, and anger, and hate. But mostly with pain. Always with pain."

She stopped, hidden by three of her biggest maples. She saw her father seated in a chair, wearing his warm fleece sweater. Across from him, Tucker sat on the grass, speaking in a soft, hesitant voice that grew stronger with each phrase.

Without a word Ginny sank down on the grass and crossed her legs, eyes riveted to Tucker's expressive face lit by the last flicker of evening light.

Every nerve of her body clenched with anticipation as she listened to him speak, watched his eyes light with a feverish glow, saw his hands clench and unclench on his knees.

He was talking about his past!

"I was only there because of my—friendship with the head of a rival faction, you know. Ulysses—that was his name. Every other journalist had been kicked out or fled to safety. But Quint and I—" his mouth creased in a rueful grin as he shook his head "—we were like two hound dogs on the scent of a skunk. We wouldn't leave, not for anything. We knew this was our turn, the chance of a lifetime. We didn't intend to mess that up."

"I see." Her father sat unmoving, his eyes closed.

Ginny, too, waited.

"It was like a scene from the Apocalypse," Tucker blurted. "Like a terrible movie being played out. Only I wasn't part of it. I was floating above it, commentating on it, directing Quint to take that shot. There were bullets ricocheting all around us, but we dashed in and out of storefronts, behind tanks, anywhere we could find shelter and grab another shot."

He stopped. Ginny could hear the rasp of his lungs as he drew in air. Beads of sweat formed on his forehead and upper lip. His fists didn't unclench at all. He seemed to be forcing the words out.

"There was some shelling, mortar fire. We ducked it by inches, but we made it to the top of a little hill, the perfect vantage spot to capture the whole scene. I yelled at Quint to pan the area, then focus on me. He argued at first, said he couldn't film me with that background, that I'd get killed."

Tucker stopped, rubbed a hand across his face. Ginny

swallowed hard when she glimpsed the tremors that shook that hand.

"I laughed at him." His voice dropped. "By then I was thinking *award*. Me, the winner of television's version of the Pulitzer. I could imagine how it would play on the six o'clock news. I insisted he stand up and film."

"That was your job, son."

Tucker ignored the interruption.

"So we shot a sequence. But the wind picked up and blasted sand across my microphone. You couldn't hear what I was saying, though the pictures told the story well enough."

He shook his head, then clasped it in both hands. His voice was so low, Ginny had to hunch forward to catch his words.

"I insisted we shoot it again. I had better words, more description, a different take. Quint was furious. He said we needed to get out of there. Just about then Ulysses came along and backed him up. He wanted us gone and he wasn't prepared to debate the subject. The whole area was going to be a pile of rubble, and we needed to get out immediately."

Tucker lurched to his feet, paced across the little clearing in jerky, odd-gaited steps, his hands thumping his thighs in an unknown rhythm.

"But I couldn't let it go. Not me. No, I knew that Quint's pictures were prize quality, you see. He'd win an award for those shots. And I wanted a share of whatever glory he would get. I was senior man, I gave the orders."

His voice fell into a calm, even rhythm, almost devoid of feeling.

"Ulysses, buddy that he was, agreed to give me five

minutes if I paid him a hundred American dollars. He
figured he could hold them off that long. If we hadn't
shot what we needed by then, we had to leave. He
promised he'd get us out safely for another hundred.''

The silence stretched so thin, Ginny was certain
they'd hear her breathing. Her body froze, but her heart
cried out to go to him, to hold him, love him. But it
was like before. She could do nothing. Nothing but
wait.

Finally Tucker spoke again.

''In the end we got only two minutes, one minute too
many as it turned out. Quint called me every name in
the book, but then he stood up and filmed exactly what
I asked for. The guns started, the mortars boomed, but
he stayed right where he was, recording it all as I said
my silly little piece.''

The breeze died. The moon, full and bright, slid out
from behind a cloud, capturing Tucker in its spotlight.
He stood, face ravaged with guilt as he finished the
story.

''I had just finished giving my name and station iden-
tification when a bullet buzzed past my ear and caught
Quint. He said, 'I've got to go, Tuck,' then tipped forward to give me the camera before he hit the ground.
He was dead. My best friend, a man I loved like a
brother, was dead. Because of me.''

Tears dripped down Ginny's face at the stark grief
she could hear. The moon was gone. Tucker stood in
the shadows, alone.

''Do you want to know what I did, Adrian?''

''You checked to see if he was still breathing.'' There
was no condemnation in her father's tone, no blame.

''Oh, yes, I did that all right.'' Tucker whirled, his

face twisted by a savage smile. "I managed that much for my *friend*."

"Good."

"Don't congratulate me! Don't act as if I did something noble. I didn't."

In a flash, the anger left, dissipated like a morning mist.

"I picked up Quint's body and carried it to the Jeep Ulysses left waiting." His mouth was a line of white, his teeth glistening. "But I made sure I had the tape."

Adrian Brown said nothing.

"Did you hear me? I was so moved by my friend's death, so traumatized by the carnage going on around me, that I had enough foresight to open that camera and grab the video so we would have something for the spot they'd held open at the station."

Tucker flopped into his lawn chair, drained of everything but loathing. He felt no relief, no cleansing, no forgiveness. The stain lay upon him, drowning him with guilt. He was no better than a murderer.

"You were hit, too, weren't you? Your eye?"

Adrian Brown studied his face, noting the faint scar lines.

"We were ambushed on the way to the Jeep. Ulysses, too." He refused to say any more, but the memories didn't stop. He winced, remembering the ragged, searing pain, the thoughts of home, of Ginny.

"So you carried Quint to the Jeep, then went back for Ulysses, ignoring your own injuries."

"Yeah." Tucker snorted, anger stinging his cheeks. "Big hero!"

"Tucker, did you ever cut yourself enough slack to

realize you were in shock? It does funny things to your mind. You don't act normally."

"Another excuse."

"Not an excuse. An explanation for grabbing the tape. You trained for years to be a reporter. It's what you've done, what you love. It became instinctive. Did you really expect yourself to act like a medic?"

"You don't get it, Adrian." Tucker forced himself to relax, to explain so the older man would see that he wasn't anything close to a hero. "We shouldn't have been there. Quint wouldn't have been there if I hadn't pushed him." The pain in his gut burned anew.

"That's true. But did you ever consider that if not for you and Quint, Ulysses might have died?"

Tucker heard the words first, then his mind absorbed them. A flicker of hope bubbled its way to the surface of his mind.

Maybe— He tamped it down.

"Ulysses wouldn't have been wounded except for me." He stood in front of Adrian. "Don't search for an excuse. There isn't one."

"Is that what this is about, Tucker? Finding an excuse for living?" Adrian pushed himself out of his chair, his face contorted with pain as he slowly straightened.

"No!" Tucker waited for Adrian to regain his breath.

"You're sure?" The older man set a gentle hand on his shoulder. "It happened, son. Just like you told young Tom. Like it or not, it's a part of your past, part of you. But it doesn't have to ruin your future."

"You were listening?" Tucker frowned.

"I'm always listening. It's the only way I learn anything." Adrian shuffled past the freshly cut stumps. "I'm going to take a pill."

"Okay."

Adrian took a few more steps, turned and held out a hand.

"Thanks for telling me."

"I can't imagine what good it could possibly have done to you to hear it." Tucker shook his hand, feeling the weakness in those tired muscles. "But you're welcome."

"Talk to yourself like you talked to Tom, son."

"I'm a better teacher than I am a student." Tucker managed a smile.

Adrian returned it. "Practice makes perfect. For teachers and students. Good night."

"Good night."

Tucker waited until Adrian had made it safely inside the house, then turned and started toward the tree house, his eyes catching a flicker of red in the evening light. He sighed.

"You can forget about sneaking past me, Ginny. I saw you hiding there." He kept right on stacking the trees they'd cut to supplement the wood the church had donated. As he worked, he waited to see what she would do.

"What can I say?" She stood, dusting off her jeans, red fuzzy slippers glowing in the night. "I take after my father. I'm always listening."

He almost laughed. That was Ginny. Brazen, straightforward, shoot-from-the-hip. And he admired that in her.

"I just have to clean this up, then I'll get out of your way."

"You're not in my way." She grabbed the end of the tree he was moving and lugged it over to the stack.

"My gorgeous trees. They were so lovely. You are going to have the boys plant more, aren't you?"

"Yeah." He twisted to look over his shoulder. "I'm sorry we had to use them, Gin. But it was that or wait until we could raise enough money to buy some more wood."

"I know." She patted the trunk lovingly. "Dear old things."

Tucker grabbed another one. "This time when we plant them, we'll avoid the geometric puzzle you created."

She didn't even argue. Instead Ginny grabbed the other end and puffed her way over to the stack he was making. She managed to continue the pace through four trees. Tucker figured it was a miracle she hadn't killed herself by then in her ridiculous wedge-heeled, slide-on slippers. He had to do something. So he claimed he needed a rest and headed for the river.

Naturally she followed.

Tucker sank down on the bank, grunting slightly when she half fell against him as she lost her balance.

"Sorry." She wiggled until she was comfortable. "I slipped."

"I wondered how long it would take."

"Don't start on my shoes again. These are my very favorites." She held out on dainty foot for him to admire.

"Lovely," Tucker told her, and meant it. "But they aren't logging shoes."

"Well, no. They're not supposed to be."

The full moon had escaped the clouds and cast its silvery glow over everything, creating a wonderland scene. How long ago Africa seemed.

"Tell me about your work, Tuck."

"Don't you think we've had enough maudlin sentiment for tonight, Gin?"

"I don't want to hear maudlin sentiment. I want to hear about where you were, what you were doing."

He searched her face, found nothing but wistful curiosity.

"I've traveled a lot," he began, then yelped at the elbow she planted in his ribs. "Well, I have!"

"Duh!" She shivered, then snuggled a little closer. "Tell me the good stuff, Tuck."

"The good stuff, huh?" He thought for a minute. "Going around the horn of South America. That was good stuff."

"How come?"

He told her about the storms they'd endured on the sailing vessel, the unusual animals, the exotic islands where Robinson Crusoe might have stopped.

"We were doing a documentary on Scottish miners traveling to Vancouver Island during the eighteen fifties. It was a rough, rugged trip, but it was gorgeous."

"Hm." She cupped her chin in her hands, her eyes huge as saucers as they gazed into the night. "What else?"

"Alaska. Oh, Gin, you've got to get up there sometime. It'll steal your breath away." He clasped her hand in his, trying to describe the majesty and wonder he'd seen. "There are caribou, Ginny. Thousands of them. They migrate across the Canadian Yukon every year. How can our government possibly think of desecrating such unspoiled beauty for an ugly thing like oil?"

"I wish I'd been there, Tuck."

"Not in those shoes, you don't." He smiled at her sniff of disgust. "You would have loved Alaska, but you wouldn't have enjoyed my next assignment, and

that's for sure, a place no one should have to see again.
Iraq, Iran, Saudi Arabia. Poor, miserable suffering souls
in a country decimated by fighting.''

He didn't tell her of the horrors. She didn't need to
know them to understand how awful it was. That was
one thing you could count on with Ginny. She understood. Her hand flicked his cheek.

"Where else, Tuck?"

"Oh, India."

"What's that like?"

"Crowded."

She shook her head at him in reproof. "Details,
Townsend. I want vivid, exotic details."

"It's hard to describe. The heat, the desperate poverty. The crowds. What bothered me most was the caste
system. Children left to fend for themselves, cardboard
shacks." He shook his head. He wouldn't go there. Tonight's memories had been dark enough.

"You'd have enjoyed the Great Barrier Reef, though."

"Australia," she whispered on a breath of awe. "Really? Tell me."

She sat there like a little girl awaiting a birthday gift,
body arched slightly toward him as she listened to his
description of the diving he'd done.

She was gorgeous. She lapped up everything, storing
it away like a squirrel hiding nuts for winter. Her face
telegraphed every emotion, and right now Ginny was
smiling.

For the sheer joy of spinning out her pleasure, Tucker
drew on every memory he could remember, pleased
when she laughed at his description of eating shark.

"I think I'd be too chicken to even try it." She turned

her shining eyes to him. "Or snake, or any of those other exotic things you mentioned."

"You should go there, Gin. Don't waste your li—"

Fool! As if she could get up and leave when her father had cancer? How stupid could he be. He clenched his fist against his leg in frustration.

Her hand covered his. Her mouth brushed against his ear in a whisper filled with certainty.

"God willing, I'll go there someday, Tucker. Not to those danger zones where you were. Not to see the poverty and desperation you covered. There's enough of that in the world."

Her arm slipped through his as she hugged him, infusing Tucker with her vision of the world.

"I want to see the awesome things, creation at its most exotic. I want to watch zebras on the veld, hear the cockatiels in their native Amazon, watch the sun never go to sleep in the Arctic."

"And then what?" He smiled into her face, caught up in her dreams.

"Then I'll come home and tell my children that God is better than they could ever dream. That He's got impeccable taste in world-making."

"Even with all the problems?"

She smiled, eyes dreamy. "God didn't make the problems on this earth. People did." She hugged him. "Oh, Tucker, thank you. Thank you for giving me this little peek into your world."

He turned his head, just a fraction to tell her she was welcome. Instead, his lips brushed hers, and Tucker was lost. His emotions had run the gamut in less than an hour, but of all the things he'd felt, Tucker knew without a doubt that he wanted to kiss Virginia Brown. She was everything fresh and wonderful, hopeful, joyful.

And just for a moment, he needed to savor her inner strength and beauty. Just for a moment he needed her strong belief in the future.

He bent his head and pressed his lips closer, twining one arm around her waist as he drew her warmth, her vibrancy, closer. For a minute he was eighteen again and life was full of delightful possibilities.

Ginny kissed him back, her soft arms clasped around his neck as if she'd never let him go.

But she did.

All at once she jerked backward, tugged herself out of his embrace.

"No."

He stared, surprised by the word. Didn't she love him anymore?

"Gin, I—" He felt like a fool. Of course she didn't love him. That was gone. He'd ruined it, like he'd ruined everything else.

"No, Tucker." She held up a hand. "I can't do this. I can't kiss you knowing that there's no meaning in it for you."

"I'm sorry—"

"You've told me often enough that the past is dead, that there is no future for us. I can't kiss you tonight and go back to being your pal in the morning. So unless something has changed—" She peered at him hopefully.

Reality hit him squarely between the eyes.

Tucker pulled his arms away, let her stand on her wobbly shoes without his help.

"I'm sorry," he whispered. "But I can't love you, Ginny. Any love I was capable of died. It was killed the day Quint died. All I have left are questions. I told—"

"You told me all of this. I know." She stood on the ridge above him, staring down. "You're wrong about love, Tucker. Totally wrong. But I'm not going to argue with you anymore."

"You're angry."

"No, I'm facing reality. For once."

He got up and walked toward the house with her, steadying her when she would have fallen.

"I've done my best to help you, to try and show you a different view of God than the one you cling to. I'll go on doing that to the best of my ability, just as I promised. But in the end, you'll only be seeing Him through my eyes just as I saw those exotic, foreign places through yours. That's not life, Tucker. That's going through the motions."

She stepped onto the deck, pulled open the screen door and smiled at him.

"There's a whole lot more of your life left, Tucker. What are you going to do with the rest of it?"

He wanted to answer her, tell her big plans, hopes, share his dreams. But he didn't have any. And anyway, she'd disappeared inside.

Tucker let himself out through the gate and strode toward the Bains', her question ringing in his head.

What was he going to do with the rest of his life?

Chapter Nine

You didn't have to go to the Arctic to watch the sun rise.

Ginny crouched in the window seat of her bedroom and sipped the steaming mug of coffee she'd just made. Iridescent pink streaks wavered across the sky, heralding the sun's ascent. It had been a long night.

Though she listened, she couldn't hear her father moving. Good. Any sleep he could manage would benefit him after the long, troubled night. Why couldn't they find whatever was wrong with him? Why was it taking so long to make a diagnosis?

As she sat there, mulling it over and praying about it, a movement on the street caught her gaze.

Tucker. Her heart hiccuped with joy in that millisecond before she could tamp it down, order it to be quiet.

He walked to the park across the street, shoulders hunkered down, obviously deep in thought. Ginny recalled his face, his words from the night before. She'd wanted to help, erase it all from his mind.

But that was impossible. Tucker didn't want her as anything more than a friend.

She accepted it now. Not happily, but with a resigned submission that burned deeply into her soul. Before she'd only said the words, but now, with her heart cold and heavy as a stony weight in her breast, she accepted that Tucker was back for a very short time. He'd find answers to the doubts, regain his beliefs, get rid of the guilt and fear and go to the next exotic location.

Someday he'd find someone he could love. But it wouldn't be her.

Ginny would be alone.

The meaning of those words stung as they penetrated from simple head knowledge and seared straight to her very soul. Her father was terribly sick. He hadn't needed to tell her. She saw it in the pale twist of his lips, in the frail shakiness of his hands. And after last night, she felt as if her father had begun to give up his struggle for life. Last night had given Ginny a foretaste of what her future would be like if he died.

Despite her brave words to Tucker, it seemed a bleak and barren forecast, one she didn't want to believe God would ask of her. But hadn't He? Even now, this morning, wasn't He giving her time to reflect on what was to come?

She watched Tucker as he climbed a tree, then sat clasped in its branches.

She loved him so much. It wasn't the same love, the bubbly high school ecstasy that blazed from her seven years ago. It had matured into a steady fire that would not be put out. She would do anything for him, give anything she possessed to see him drop that mantle of pain and regain his relationship with God, even if it meant she never saw him again.

Are you truly willing to practice real love—to give everything you can to him with no thought of gain? Is your love big enough to let him go?

Ginny flinched at the thought. Let Tucker go? Let him walk away without ever telling him how much she longed to fulfill the promise he'd made? Put away her dreams of a future together and never resurrect them again?

Agonized tears filled her eyes.

Is that what you ask of me, Lord? It's too hard.

Tucker swung himself down from the tree, his motions rough, angry. He kicked a stone out of the road, then stalked off down the street, his back toward her.

His pain was like a physical sword that reached out and pierced her heart. Was having her way, getting Tucker to stay here, even if it made him miserable—was any of that worth the cost to him?

As she sat listening to the birds drenching the morning with their song, Ginny counted the cost of letting Tucker Townsend go. Of never kissing him again. Of never having his child, never riding his motorbike, never sharing his achievements. She forced herself to picture endless evenings sitting in this house, alone.

Then a new vision swept into her mind. Tucker, in a cathedral somewhere far across the sea, lifting his face to heaven as he knelt to worship—a beautiful, pain-free countenance that shone with the wonder and glory of the God who'd forgiven him.

He's my child, Ginny. I love him more than you can even imagine.

The truth of it washed over her like a smooth soft blanket of peace. She had to let go. It would hurt. It would be the most painful thing she'd ever done. But Tucker was worth it.

"All right, Father. I'll take each day You give me, each golden moment You allow me to share with Dad and Tucker, and use them the best I can. I won't ask for more than You're willing to give. All I ask is that You be there. Always."

The sun was completely free of the horizon, lifting into the sky in blazing brilliance, bathing her in a warm wash of heavenly comfort.

Ginny stared out her window for a long time until a heavenly peace eased some of her hurt. Then she turned and prepared for the day the Lord had given.

"We'd like to know when you think you might return. Not that we're rushing you, of course. You're entitled to take all the time you need to heal. You certainly deserve it."

The phone call from last night would not be silenced.

Tucker stalked home, disgusted by the way his mind cringed in the face of this recall. He'd turned them down, of course. Just as he had last week. Just as he would next week.

"The network is happy to cover any further medical treatment you might need, Tucker. They know you put your life on the line to get that coverage."

Not only his own life. But nobody ever said that out loud.

"We've got a story just waiting for you, if you're interested."

Tucker wasn't interested. Not in the least. So he'd stalled them, lied that his eye wasn't yet up to par. It wasn't perfect, true. But he could have managed. He'd used it long enough to get another column ready for Marty's paper last week. No, it wasn't the eye.

If he understood the reasons God had done that awful

thing, if he could figure out why God let him down so badly, recapture that tenuous thread enough to start a relationship with the Almighty, he could have gone back.

But not yet.

Jubilee Junction didn't boast the danger or excitement he was used to, but at least here he was in control of his fate. Here one misstep wouldn't cost someone his life. Here he was safe.

Tucker walked into the Bains' house and reluctantly joined the couple for breakfast. Not that the food wasn't good, but he felt uncomfortable during their devotions. Lately his former coach had taken to reading passages about forgiveness. Deliberately, Tucker was certain.

He tucked his head onto his chest, listened to the verses, the prayers that followed, then helped clear the table.

"You going to give Ginny a hand in the store today?" Coach snuck another cinnamon roll off the plate and scurried out the door before his wife caught him.

"Give her a hand? Why?" Why would Ginny need his help?

Coach shrugged, savored a big hunk of cinnamon sugar, then finally spoke.

"Saw the lights on at their house last night when I took the dog out. Doc's car went past during breakfast, and she was up when I went running this morning."

Coach ran every morning at six. Tucker knew something was wrong.

"Her father?" He remembered the news Adrian had shared yesterday and caught his breath.

"I'm guessing. Didn't look too good yesterday when I stopped by, but I doubt if he told Ginny how poorly he was feeling."

Tucker doubted she knew, either. He didn't know what to do. On the one hand he felt Ginny should be prepared, but on the other, Adrian's words were said in confidence.

"I think I will stop by the store, offer a hand. There must be odd jobs I could do."

Tucker hurried upstairs, anxious to find a clean shirt and another pair of pants. As he combed his hair, he saw his reflection and realized that for once, he felt a sense of purpose. At last he'd found something he could do. That, and maybe, just maybe, he'd write another column. At least it would keep him busy. And maybe it would atone, at least partially, for his other mistake.

"Hey, man, where are you going? This tree house ain't half finished!" Tom's eyes stared as Tucker began storing the tools he'd borrowed from the coach.

"I know, but it's all I can do for tonight. I've got to write a column."

"A column? Why?"

Tucker couldn't very well tell him the truth, that he'd been dared into it. Or couldn't he?

"Because your foster father promised he'd do something very nasty if I didn't fill the space he's got left because he didn't plan properly." He winked at Tom.

"That's a lie!" Marty dropped the can of nails on the floor and scurried down the ladder. "You promised you'd do it. Now you're trying to welch like some hotshot reporter who's too good for the local rag." Marty's grin dared him to rebut that.

"Am not."

"Big hero! Is my paper too petty for you?"

Ouch! That one stung until Tucker caught the glint in Marty's eye. Ah, he was showing off.

They argued good-naturedly for a while. Tom's head swiveled from left to right, watching.

"You guys can make a big deal out of anything," he muttered, raking a hand through his sawdust-covered hair. "What's so hard about writing a dinky little column? It's not like you haven't been enough places, Tucker."

"Yeah." Marty grinned as he patted his foster son on the back. "You tell him, son."

"And you, you're just the same. Moaning every single morning about how you're too old to be running a newspaper, how you should be retired." Tom shook his head in disgust. "Man! It's not like people actually depend on you for the news, Marty. They can tune in Tucker's channel anytime and find out what's happening in the world."

Marty's mouth dropped to his chest in consternation.

Tom missed that because he bent to pick up some fallen nails. "I mean, it's a newspaper, guys. No big deal, okay?"

"No big deal?" Tucker blinked. "Did you hear that, Marty? This little brat thinks our work is no big deal."

"I heard."

Marty looked so pained by the admission, Tucker almost laughed. But one glance at Tom kept his lips straight.

"I think it's time for some formal education for our little friends, don't you?" An idea stirred in the back of Tucker's brain.

"What did you have in mind?"

Tucker drew Marty away from the kids who'd come over to see what was going on. He laid out his idea in a few choice words, then stepped back to see what his friend would say. A huge smile covered Marty's face. His eyes sparkled with fun.

"Education's wonderful," he agreed, clapping Tucker on the back. He winked, then turned toward Tom. "Since a mind is a terrible thing to waste, let's consider that school's in, boys. Get that stuff put away. We're heading over to the paper."

"But I thought we didn't have enough cash to finish the wings on the plane?" Paul and Kent looked to the rest for an explanation of the grown-ups' odd behavior.

"We don't." Tucker grinned. He could hardly wait to see what these smart-aleck kids did with his latest brain wave.

"So?" Ira, John and Nick joined in, their faces blank. "What're we gonna do at the paper?"

"You'll see."

Tucker lugged Coach's tool kit through the yard, passing Ginny on the way. She carried a tray with cans of soda piled on top and a plate with that cereal dessert she made—the one with butterscotch, chocolate and peanut butter topping. He licked his lips. On his way back to the tree house, he found her waiting for him.

"Quitting kind of early, aren't you?" She smiled as brightly as usual, but there were tired lines around her eyes. A droop of weariness sloped her shoulders.

Tucker knew she was worn out from the runs to the city. Her father had been admitted to the cancer center for tests two days ago, and she'd been forcing herself to make the round trip every evening. Tucker had gone with her to keep her company. Last night Adrian had insisted they both take a night off.

"We're going over to the paper," he told her quietly. "Since we've gone as far as we can go with the plane, and because the boys expressed an interest in journalism, Marty and I figured we'd see if they were interested enough to try to print their own club newspaper."

She looked at him admiringly. "Wow!"

He shrugged.

"We've had six new kids join, you know. They can't all come every night to the clubhouse like the original group because some of them need rides in from their farms, but if we do the paper, we might work something out for Saturday afternoons."

"Can I come, too?"

In the act of turning away, Tucker froze, then twisted back to stare at her.

"Come? With us? To the paper?"

"Uh-huh."

"What for?"

"Bad idea." She turned away. "Never mind."

He reached out and grabbed her arm, stopping her.

"No, wait. I didn't say it was a bad idea."

"You didn't exactly welcome me with open arms, either."

If she meant something by those particular words, if she was harking back to his promise, Tucker couldn't tell it by looking at her. She stood in front of him, slim, quiet, totally unlike the usual bouncy Ginny. Even her hair was restrained in its thick braid.

Automatically, his gaze slipped to her feet. Sure enough, he found what he needed to reassure him that Ginny, the real Ginny, was still alive and kicking.

She wore some kind of straps—no, maybe they were laces. They started at the sides of her feet and went back and forth across her instep. They were attached to lime-green soles. There seemed to be six straps on each side, and they crisscrossed in some kind of intricate pattern that mystified him. Above her ankle, the laces wrapped around her leg and tied in neat bows. If these were supposed to be shoes, he'd never seen anyone else wear them.

She followed his stare.

"Do you like them?" She lifted one leg fractionally higher so he could get a better look. "I ordered them from a catalogue. They're an absolute pain to fasten, but once you get them on, they're really comfortable."

"Uh-huh." Tucker wasn't going to go there. He focused on her face. "If you want to come, Gin, you're more than welcome."

"Ask the boys first," she suggested. "They may not want me tagging along."

Tucker turned to stare at his kids, who were happily swallowing soda as they grabbed for the delectable squares.

"As if!" He shook his head at her. "Bribery always works with them. Especially if it's food."

She grinned, shrugged.

"We mere women do what we can," she murmured demurely.

He burst out laughing at her faked submissively prissy face and kept on laughing on the inside while she charmed each and every one of them into coaxing her along. Once at the newspaper building, they vied for her attention, edging each other out.

"You guys want to know how difficult it is to make a newspaper, you're going to find out," Marty told them, grinning like a Cheshire cat once he'd finished the tour of the building and explanations as to their presence.

"Yeah? How?" Tom frowned.

"Each of you are to write a column, no more, no less than five hundred words, on any subject you want."

"Huh?" They stared at him in utter confusion.

"We're going to put out our very own newspaper, guys." Tucker grinned, enjoying their stunned surprise. "Each of you is going to contribute something to it. If you don't want to do a column, think of something else. But have it here Saturday morning."

"I don't know how to write a stupid old column." Tom glared at his foster father as if he'd betrayed him. "What would I write about, anyhow?"

"Your life before you came here, your family, what you want the club to be about, things you want to do in the future. You name it. We're open." Marty didn't back down from Tom's glare. "You said it was easy. Let's see how you handle this one little part of building a newspaper."

"How're we going to pay to get the stuff printed?"

Tucker nodded. "Good question, Nick. Any suggestions?"

They stared at him as if he'd grown two heads.

"Sell it."

Ginny's words had them all twisting to stare at her.

"Who's going to buy a kids' newspaper?" The entire group started guffawing at the very idea.

"Well, that will depend on you. Make it interesting enough and I think lots of kids would want to see what this club of yours is about."

In three seconds she'd captured their imaginations, painting a picture they'd never be able to resist. Tucker watched her surreptitiously. It didn't matter who Ginny Brown talked to, she couldn't help encouraging them. Her beauty was stunning enough, but the essence of Ginny was her indomitable spirit. She just refused to quit.

"Hey, that's not bad." Tom was grinning, his eyes

sparkling with ideas. "Somebody needs to write up a report of our meeting and our plans for the next one." He nodded as one boy raised his hand. "Okay. And we should have an explanation about our odd-job squad, you know, how we're going to buy a motor for the plane."

Another boy volunteered.

"Kent, why don't you sketch some cartoons? You can draw way better than you can write. Nick's good on computers. He could set up the headings and that stuff."

Marty thunked Tucker in the ribs.

"Look at him," he murmured. "The kid's a born organizer."

Tucker nodded. In a matter of ten minutes, each boy had an assignment they seemed to accept far better than being told to write a column. Once more, they'd taken an idea and made it their own. Watching them change from takers to givers gave Tucker intense pleasure.

"Hey, you got us all lined up. What're you gonna do?" The other boys nodded, staring at Tom.

"I think he should be the editor-in-chief." Ginny stood straight and tall in her lace-up shoes. "He's already doing that, anyway."

"Aw, I dunno." Tom's face turned a bright red. "I'm no good at this stuff."

"You're perfect. Marty? Tucker?" Her eyes asked for support.

Tucker caught a glimpse of rebellion on more than one face. He spoke before Marty could.

"It's up to them. It's their paper." He motioned to the other two adults. "Let's go outside while they discuss it."

They climbed the stairs and stepped out the back

door, surprising someone who'd been standing at a nearby window.

"Hey, you!" Tucker sprinted after a disappearing figure, grabbed him by the shoulder. "What are you doing?"

"Nothing!"

"It's Lane, isn't it?" Ginny moved closer to get a better look under the street lamp. "I thought I recognized you. Let him go, Tucker. He won't run away."

Reluctantly Tucker removed his hand, hoping Ginny knew what she was doing. The kid looked like a punk with his weird hair and scruffy clothing. But then, Lane probably didn't look any worse than the other kids in the group. Tucker was just used to them.

"I suppose you're wondering about the boy's club," she said when Lane didn't say anything. "Do you want to join?"

"I dunno. What kinda things do they do?" He slouched, staring at her insolently.

"You can ask them yourself. They'll be out soon. They'll have to be. They have curfews."

He snorted with disgust at the word, but backed down when she reminded him that he had one, too. How did she come by all this information? Tucker stood and listened, amazed at her skill with kids.

A few minutes later the boys emerged.

"We voted to let Tom be the editor. He's the oldest and he can spell better than the rest of us, so we figured he'd be better at it." Nick spoke for the group. "Who's this?"

"This is Lane. He's thinking about joining the group." Ginny introduced everyone.

"I might be interested and I might not." Lane tugged a pack of cigarettes out of his shirt and flicked one into his mouth. He lit it with a match, which he immediately tossed away.

"We've got rules. One is no smoking. We're not allowed. It's part of probation. Besides, John's allergic."

"That so?" Lane inhaled deeply, then blew the smoke directly into John's face.

Tucker jerked forward, itching to rush to the weakly boy's defense when he started coughing. Ginny grabbed his arm and held him back.

"Watch," she whispered.

"You know, kid, you've got a problem. But then, I guess we all do." Tom stepped in front of John, his shoulders straight, eyes keen. "That's why we're in this club. But when we're in this club, we're all equal and nobody's a hotshot. We might have done some stupid things in the past, but we're not aiming to repeat the experience. This is our chance to make good, and we're going to do it together, as a group."

"Yeah." The rumble of agreement rolled through the ranks as the other boys backed Tom up.

"So you're only letting certain people in, is that it?"

"Nope." Tom shook his head. "Anybody's welcome. But we all have to follow the rules because the rules benefit everyone. You wanna join, you follow them just like the rest of us. The choice is up to you."

Lane flicked his cigarette out of his fingers and onto the ground, cheeks hot with embarrassment when Tom stepped forward and ground the cigarette's burning end into the dust with his heel.

"This Hicksville Goody Two-shoes junk isn't for me." Lane glared at Tom. "You're a bunch of sissies. I wouldn't be part of this bunch for nothing!"

Tom shrugged.

"Suit yourself. You're welcome anytime, though. As long as you follow our rules."

"I won't be back. So you can stuff your rules!" Lane sauntered away without looking back.

Ginny wiggled a little, and Tucker realized with a start that she stood in the circle of his arm. Somehow one of his hands had moved around her shoulder. He hadn't even noticed, she fit so naturally. Reluctantly he removed his hand.

"I'm glad he's gone. He's mean."

The others began to describe the things they'd heard about Lane. Tom held up a hand.

"Hey, look. None of us is exactly pure as the driven snow. If we can change, he can, too. Let's give him a chance to think it over, okay?"

"It's time you fellows were on your way home." Marty stepped up, smiling. "I guess you've got your assignments, so we'll see you Saturday morning. 10:00 a.m."

"See you."

They hurried away into the evening. Tucker turned, surprised to see that Tom remained behind, speaking softly to Ginny. He stepped closer to listen.

"I didn't do it for them," the boy explained, his face absolutely serious. "I did it for me. I needed to give somebody else a break. After all, I got one." He glanced at Tucker and grinned. "You're the one who showed me that it doesn't matter where you come from, you can make something out of your life."

"I did?" Tucker shifted uncomfortably, glimpsing the hero worship in the boy's eyes. "I didn't do anything but help Marty get you guys together. Seems to me you've done the rest on your own."

Tom shook his head.

"I got Marty to let me look up some stuff on microfiche. I know all about you carrying your friend's body out, then going back for the other guy. And you were injured."

Tucker's breath got stuck in his throat. He couldn't say a word. The last thing he wanted was some kind of misplaced hero worship from a kid who needed a role model. But what could he do? If he told the truth, Tom would tell the boys, and then it would be all over town—the real truth of the matter.

"That's the kind of man I'm going to be," Tom said, face filled with pride. "I'm going to make a difference in my world. A difference for good. I decided tonight when I saw how badly that kid wanted to belong to our group. That was me not so long ago, you know. Tough talking, mean. But inside I was shriveled up. I figured out that to do what Tucker did, you've got to be looking outside yourself. That's what I'm going to do—I'm going to be a reporter, just like Tucker."

Tucker froze. Be like him? Please God, not that!

"I'm glad, Tom. I think that's a wonderful plan and I believe you'll make a big difference." Ginny hugged him for a minute, then let him go, grinning at his red face. "Get going now before you're late."

"I've got to lock up. I'll see you later, Tom." Marty watched the boy leave, his chest puffed out in obvious pride. "At least we've made a dent in turning one kid around."

Tucker nodded, muttered something and left Marty to close up shop. He started down the sidewalk, unsurprised when Ginny fell into step beside him.

"That was a good plan," she congratulated him. "Now they're pulling together. It's easier to stand up for something when there's more than one."

"Did you hear him, Gin?" Tucker agonized over the remembered words. "He wants to be like me. What a gross mistake that would be!"

"But you're a wonderful reporter and usually a very nice man." She grinned. The smile drooped, then faded as she realized he was serious. "Why wouldn't he want to emulate you?"

"Because I'm a liar and a cheat." There—he'd said it. "Tom thinks I'm some kind of hero, Gin. He doesn't know the truth."

"So tell him."

She said it so simply, as if it were the easiest thing in the world to admit you were a flop at life.

"And wreck the trust and faith he's put in me? Have it blabbed all over town?" He shook his head. "No. I can't."

"Is it your reputation you're worried about, Tuck?"

He stopped, stared at her.

"Of course it's my reputation. I've spent a long time becoming tops in my field."

"And being the top—is that enough for you? Wouldn't you give up your reputation, your job, everything, to be at peace inside yourself? What is it you're trying so hard to prove, Tucker? And who are you trying to prove it to?"

"What do you mean?"

When she suddenly veered left, Tucker realized they had arrived at her house. He walked her to the door, his mind turning over what she'd said.

"Why do you think I'm trying to prove anything?"

"Because you refuse to accept that God loves you, that He forgives you, that He is willing to accept you just the way you are. It's as if you're trying to buy yourself into His good graces, to atone for your mistakes. You can't do that any more than Lane could keep smoking and be part of the group.''

He frowned, ready to argue.

But Ginny opened the door and slipped inside, her muffled good-night barely discernible.

She was wrong, of course. Dead wrong. It didn't have to do with atoning for the past, it had to do with making sure it never happened again. And until he got that promise from God, he wasn't going out into a world where he got his friends killed.

Chapter Ten

On Sunday afternoon three weeks later, Ginny sat beside Tucker in her car, grateful that he hadn't insisted on riding his motorbike to visit her father. She needed reassurance.

"I'm sure we'll find him much better." Tucker drove smoothly, easing around traffic as they moved into the city.

"I hope so. This is the third time he's been in here in three weeks. I just wish they'd diagnosed the appendicitis ages ago. Surely it's a routine thing with stomach pain?"

"Well, nothing showed up on the tests, and his symptoms weren't exactly routine, Gin. Besides, that combined with his history of gallbladder problems, and the spastic colon attacks he started showing at the first..." Tucker shook his head. "I guess it was just too many things all at the same time."

"I know. He couldn't clearly identify the location of his pain, and that kind of threw them off, too. Still, I hope we're done with all this doctoring now. It's getting expensive." She frowned at the fleeting look that washed over Tucker's face, then disappeared. "What?"

"Nothing." He smiled at her. "I guess I'm just relieved that it wasn't the cancer he feared so much. When they ruled that out, I know he felt a whole lot better."

"Until he had that last attack." She closed her eyes. "That was awful."

"I know." He squeezed her hand for a moment, remembering. "Perhaps that's why he put off coming here for so long, telling you that the pain was different, that it had moved. He was afraid."

"If I know my father, you're right on target." Ginny nodded. "And that fear convinced him to do nothing for far too long. I should have insisted on bringing him in immediately. I shouldn't have listened to him." She touched Tucker's arm. "I never did thank you properly for spending so much time running back and forth to visit him. I know it shortened up his days."

"It was the least I could do. Besides, coming to see your dad was more like consulting a wise owl than visiting someone in the hospital. He has good advice."

"Except when it pertains to himself." She grimaced, pushing away the memory of the fear and worries of the past weeks. She tried to hide a yawn, but it was too much work. When she opened her eyes, Tucker was staring at her.

"Are you all right?"

"You're the one I should be asking that," she told him. "You and Marty had a pretty late night, I take it."

"Who squealed?" He studied her for a minute, considering. "Marty's wife?" he guessed at last.

"She phoned around midnight, looking for her missing husband. I think you two need a curfew more than the kids.''

Tucker grinned. "Maybe. But those kids are doing superb work. The first newspaper is a smash. We've run off three batches. Everybody in town seems curious about our little group."

"I know." Should she tell him of the worries that were circulating through the Chamber of Commerce after several recent vandalism incidents? "Are they getting more odd jobs?" she asked, putting off the inevitable.

"Some." He shrugged. "It's hard to gauge what people are thinking, though I've heard complaints about problem kids influencing the local boys. I can't control what people say. I can only help the boys do the best they can. If people won't accept their efforts, it's their loss."

"It would be nice if some of the local kids joined your group. That would put an end to the rumors."

"Actually, we've got a couple. Not choirboys, by any means, but they're pulling their weight. I've even seen Lane hanging around, giving us a second look."

"Which may be good or bad, depending on his attitude." Ginny grinned. "Running this group—it's not the easiest job in the world, is it?"

"It's harder than anything I've ever done," he told her with feeling.

Ginny grinned. "But worth it?"

His voice, when he finally spoke, was quiet. "I hope so. I've certainly butted some heads trying to get the community to accept what we're doing."

He drove in silence for several minutes.

"It might be an idea to take the boys to a town council meeting and let the powers that be see how serious these kids are about their club.'' She thought for a minute, trying to conceive of a way to set fears at rest. ''Maybe the boys could do a profile of each member with each paper.''

Tucker stared at her for so long, Ginny wondered if he'd forgotten he was driving.

''How do you come up with this stuff?'' he demanded. ''I have to contemplate for hours before I get an idea, and you just roll them off. It's very annoying.''

Ginny grinned. ''Sorry.'' She debated whether or not to ask, but eventually decided nothing lost, nothing gained. ''Mrs. Bains told me the network's been after you,'' she said tentatively.

Tucker jerked upright as if he'd been burned.

''Yeah, they called a couple of times.'' His tone didn't invite questions.

Ginny asked anyway. ''Are you going back?''

''Not yet,'' he snapped.

''Tucker—''

''Look, Gin. It's all a mess.'' His hand slapped the steering wheel in disgust.

''Tell me,'' she murmured.

''They're giving me an award. A man died, another was injured, and they're giving me an award.'' He laughed, but there was no mirth in it. ''I don't want it. I don't even want to hear about it. And I'm sure as heck not going back to accept it.''

''But—'' She stopped the words, but not soon enough. His eyes flashed to hers, pain lurking in their depths.

''But that was what I wanted, isn't that what you were going to say, Ginny? That's why I pushed so hard to get the story in the first place—to get that award and the kudos that go along with it. Isn't that what you were thinking?''

"Not exactly. I was going to say that by accepting their award you could have paid some tribute to Quint. Presumably there is coverage when this award is made?''

He nodded. "Tons.''

"Couldn't you ask them to hold off announcing it until you're back so you could receive it personally?''

"I guess.'' He kept his eyes averted. "The thing is, that award brings it all back. The bonus I'd been promised, the prestige winning that award would bring, the hype my boss would toss out to the head honcho about me—I can't help remembering that's why I insisted on those shots, to get all that.''

Ginny took a deep breath.

"You know, Tucker, I never took you for the kind of man who pities himself.''

"What?'' His eyes blazed with anger when he turned his head to glare at her. "What are you talking about?''

"Your power trip. You keep going on and on about being to blame, but you never bother to look inside yourself, to dig a little deeper for your own motives.''

"What motives?'' he demanded suspiciously. "I was greedy. What more is there to it?''

"Actually I think there's quite a lot more to this whole thing, and I think you're avoiding the truth.''

"Keep going.'' His cheek twitched with a nerve that signaled the tight control he exerted on himself. "You've said this much, don't stop now.''

"I wasn't going to.'' She tilted her chin, then said the words he needed to hear. "Think about what you do in relation to the rest of us, Tucker. If you hadn't shown us the inhumanity, the suffering, the starvation, how long would it have gone on?''

''There are other—''

''Our project, the one we started just after you came to town, that wouldn't have come about if we hadn't seen your report. Now, thanks to everyone's efforts, we have almost enough money collected to make a difference in some lives.'' Ginny could see she wasn't getting through. She prayed for help as she spoke, choosing her next words with great care.

''God used you, Tucker, even though you didn't realize it. Far from abandoning you, He may have sent you to that very place simply to show the rest of us, sitting comfortably in our safe, middle-class homes, the awful lives of children in those war-torn countries. Who is to know? Who can discern God's reasons?''

''He could have spared Quint's life. He could have sent us somewhere else.'' The harsh, angry words seemed to spill out in spite of himself.

''He could have, but He didn't. Think about that, Tuck. Why didn't He? Maybe there's something God is trying to show you.''

''Now you're trying to tell me these doubts, this fear—it's all on purpose?'' He blinked, as if he couldn't believe what he'd heard.

''Maybe. I don't know.'' She stopped, thought for a moment, then glared at him. ''Don't feed me that stuff about God abandoning you, Tucker. He doesn't, it's that simple. He just uses different ways and means to wake us up.''

''Different?'' He nodded once, his tone sarcastic. ''Yeah, that's for sure.''

Ginny wanted to let it go, wanted to forget trying to prod him to reconsider the reason for his problems. But she couldn't. She would say the words that pressed to be spoken, then she'd let Tucker deal with it.

"He's shifted your world, thrown you out of your comfort zone. Ask yourself why. And don't settle for quick answers."

He said nothing more as they reached the outskirts of the city, and neither did Ginny. It was up to God now. She'd said what He put on her mind. Perhaps Tucker would find the answers he sought.

As for her, she had to concentrate on her father. She prayed that this time he'd be able to stay at home, to recover, to share the future with her. Because once Tucker left Jubilee Junction, her father was all she had left.

As Tucker parked in the vast lot, Ginny gathered her courage around her and prayed for peace. Then she opened her car door and stepped onto the pavement.

The lot was almost empty. The usual Sunday afternoon visitors had not yet arrived. They crossed the tarmac, entered the building and snagged an elevator with no problem, whirring up to the fifth floor in a matter of seconds. The door to Adrian's room was shut.

Ginny took a deep breath, whispered a plea for help, then pasted a smile on her face. She tapped once, then shoved the door open and waltzed inside as if the cares of the world had flown away.

"Hi, Daddy."

Her father sat, fully clothed, in a big armchair beside the window. His suitcase lay at his feet.

Ginny stared. "What's all this, Dad?"

He accepted her kiss and hug, returned it with a weaker version of his own, then nodded at Tucker.

"Hi, honey. Tucker. They're releasing me today. I

told them not to call you, that you were coming anyway. I'm ready to go.''

"So soon? Are you sure you're strong enough?'' She checked the pallor of his face and found it remarkably improved.

"I feel better than I have in years, Ginny. Just a little sore where the incision is, but that will be gone in no time. I can hardly wait to get back to work.'' He glanced from Tucker to Ginny. He flashed a teasing smile at Ginny. "I've already heard what he did with my display at the store. There's no point pretending the place doesn't need me. Half the town's been talking.''

"Maybe. But neither is there any reason for you to think you're going to waltz out of here and straight into the store.'' Ginny crossed her arms over her chest. "If that's what you think, you can stay here another week.''

"No way! I'm sick to death of tea, yellow Jell-O and apple juice.''

Ginny gave him a look she'd often used to quell the boys. It seemed to work. Her father sighed.

"All right, I'll take it easy. The truth is, I'm so glad to have that pain gone, I'll be thrilled just to get a good night's sleep in my own bed.''

"Oh. I see your visitors have arrived.'' The nurse breezed into the room with a cheery smile. "Aren't you the lucky one?''

Adrian rolled his eyes and muttered, "Oh, very lucky.'' He raised his voice, pretending he was talking to Tucker. "Do you know that the staff in this place actually wake you up to ask if you are asleep?''

The nurse sniffed at this remark, handed Adrian a form to sign, then turned to Ginny.

"He's very hard to please.'' She grinned, her back to Adrian, voice severe. "Always ringing for something or other. We have sick people here, you know, Mr. Brown. We can't afford to have old men lollygagging around.''

"Old? Me?"

They bickered back and forth good-naturedly, then the nurse read the doctor's instructions.

"Next time you feel ill, get it checked immediately. I know you like to get your money's worth, Mr. Brown, but I think this time you carried things to the extreme.'' She pulled a wheelchair into the room. "And you're too old for extreme anything," she teased. "All ready?"

He began to protest, insisted he'd rather walk, but she cut him off.

"Mr. Brown, it is within my power to arrange for your visit with us to be extended. Do you want to test me on this?"

Adrian pursed his lips, got into the wheelchair and rode silently to the entrance. The nurse hugged him goodbye, grinned at them all, then scooted off down the hallway, whistling as she went.

"She's got your number, Dad." Ginny couldn't help but laugh.

"I thought she was nice." Tucker shifted the suitcase, offering his arm to Adrian.

"She is a great nurse. But for all her smiles, she doesn't take any guff." Adrian walked the short distance to the car with no problem. "I kind of like that about her. Though I'd never tell her so. She'd jump at the chance to keep me in there, you know."

"We gathered." Ginny shared a grin with Tucker.

"I'd like to stop someplace for lunch," Adrian told them once everyone was settled inside the vehicle. "I'm starved. Yellow Jell-O at six a.m. does not stick to the ribs.''

Ginny couldn't talk him out of it, so she gave up trying. Tucker found a restaurant with a Sunday brunch that let Adrian to choose the foods the doctors allowed.

Ginny dawdled over food she didn't really want, content to listen to her father and Tucker exchange information. This was what she'd always wanted—the three of them sharing their day, being together. It was what she'd spent years dreaming of, hoping for, trusting God to deliver. But Tucker's confirmation that the network wanted him back made this moment bittersweet.

What had she done wrong to lose that dream? Had she simply been naive to trust so easily, or was it because she'd never stopped to question that her dream was not God's dream? Had she misread God's will for them seven years ago? And if so, how could she understand it now? Were her desires and motivations pushing her off the course God had designed?

''You're quiet, Gin.'' Tucker sat sipping the last of his coffee while they waited for her father to return to the table. ''Are you all right?''

''I'm fine. Tired, I guess. Wondering.''

''About what?'' He set the cup down, his attention firmly centered on her.

Ginny took a deep breath. Maybe this wasn't the place, maybe it wasn't the time. But she was going to say it anyway. She was tired of fighting her doubts alone.

''About the past. About the future. About God's will for me.''

''I thought you had that all mapped out.'' He frowned at her. ''Don't you?''

''Tucker, I'm no different than you.'' Ginny couldn't

help smiling. "I'm curious about why things happen. I'd like to know when my prayers will be answered, what's in the future." She suppressed the tremble in her voice. "I guess I'm feeling a little anticlimactic today."

"No, that isn't it." He seemed to sense her uncertainty and reached out to cover her hands with his. "Tell me what's wrong."

"I'm wondering if I've been doing the things I've been doing with the wrong motives." She could see that he didn't understand. "For instance—did I stay in Jubilee Junction with Dad because it was my duty or because I loved him?"

Tucker snorted. "Because you loved him and wanted to help, of course." He said it as if there were no other possible answer.

"I'm not so sure. I could have gone to college, Tuck. Dad would have managed. He'd even have cheered me on. Why didn't I take the chance, step out in faith?" She tried to remember what had gone into that decision. "After the first year, once we got into a routine, I didn't have to be there. Someone else could have done what I did."

Tucker shook his head, his eyes glowing with admiration. "I doubt that, Gin. I don't think anyone could ever do what you do."

She smiled, loving him more now than she ever had. Tucker, who battled his own problems, was so certain of her faith. Why wasn't she? Why was she suddenly doubting what she'd trusted in for so long?

"That's a nice thing to say, but it's not true. Dad could have trained anyone. Was I so naive that I thought I was the only one who could be there for him?" She hesitated, then spoke from her heart. "If I'd gone, Dad might have found someone else to love."

She glanced at her father, who stood several tables away, talking to a friend he'd known for years.

"Now I wonder if my staying was simply a selfish response, a way to avoid plunging into a world I knew nothing about, a world in which I could fail. Maybe I took the easy way out."

Tucker would be leaving soon, moving on to another job, another country, another tragedy. She would lose him again, and the knowledge ate at her. If only she hadn't stayed behind seven years ago. If only she'd pursued her dream with him.

"You listen to me, Ginny Brown." He tilted her chin so he could look directly into her eyes. "You stayed in the Junction because you trusted me to keep my word. That was your biggest mistake, but trusting me was the only one you made. It's one I can't ever make up for. You wasted seven years on me and you'll never get them back."

"No, I—"

One finger pressed against her lips.

"But you never wasted your time in Jubilee, not one single moment. You didn't stay because you were selfish, or scared, or because you wanted your own way. You stayed because you saw a need and you had to fill it. That's who you are. That's what you are."

"Is it?" She smiled through the tears that filled her eyes. "Maybe you don't know me as well as you think, Tucker."

"I know you better than you know yourself. Do you think I'm not aware of your feelings? Do you honestly believe that I don't know you'd like us to be what we were before?" He brushed a tear from her cheek, his voice throbbing with emotion. "I know it, Gin. I knew it from the start, just as I knew you'd put your own needs on hold if you thought there was a chance of helping me out of my mental dungeon. I was even so bad off, I counted on it."

"But you don't feel that way?" Would hope never die?

Tucker shook his head firmly, without hesitation.

"No. I can't. I won't put you through that again." He tried to soften his words. "I'm not the kind of man you need, Ginny. I'm a traveler. I traipse across the world in pursuit of a story, endangering myself, my friends, everyone, for the sake of fame and fortune." His lips turned down. "As a husband, I'm a write-off, Gin. You can do a lot better."

"Then what you're really saying is that coming here, to me, hasn't helped you at all." She risked a glance at him, her eyes welling with tears at the agreement she found. "And that's exactly what I meant. I'm only kidding myself by pretending I'm doing any good here."

The truth smacked her between the eyes. She'd said the words in her prayers, pretending she was leaving it all up to God, but her heart still clung to a dream—one where Tucker loved her. A silly, stupid, childish, happily-ever-after dream.

"Why do you say that? Because you can't make my nightmare go away?" He smiled, but the smile was sad, full of yearning. "You're only human, Gin. You can't control everyone and everything. You can't always make it better, though you've tried harder than most."

"Coming back here, talking, it hasn't helped you at all?" She desperately needed to know the answer.

"I don't have any answers, no. And I still have a lot of questions."

It was only when he pulled his hand away that Ginny realized how tightly she'd clung to it. He leaned back in his chair, his face rueful, his fingers unconsciously tapping on the table.

"I feel like I'm marking time. There's nothing I'd like more than to hightail it out of here, put an end to this waiting. I want to figure things out and get on with my life. But I can't. Something you said got to me, made me think that if God is really in control, there had to be a reason for Quint's death." He sighed. "I'm afraid to move on until I figure out what that reason was. Then maybe I won't make the same mistake again."

"You're still saying it was your fault?"

He nodded. "I can't get away from that." He hunched forward, his face grave. "I was obsessed, Ginny. As I look back, I don't remember much of anything but the hunt, the pursuit of another story, another headline, another bonus."

"A lot of people are workaholics," she offered, trying to ease his suffering.

"No, it was far beyond that. Work was my god, and I couldn't satisfy it, no matter how hard I tried." His eyes grew hazy, faded into something from the past that he did not share.

Ginny studied him, her mind whirring. When she spoke, it was slowly, thoughtfully. She searched for each word, certain he was on the right track but not sure how to proceed.

"Perhaps you need to figure out why you became so obsessed. What drove you, Tucker? What made becoming a success so important to you?"

He frowned, obviously unsure of her meaning.

Ginny would have expounded further, but her father came back. After that, they left the restaurant. On the drive home, she decided that perhaps it was better this way, better to let Tucker sort through it for himself, find his own answers.

She certainly didn't have any. In fact, her mind was filled with questions. Why had she spent seven long years believing in something that so obviously was not going to happen? When she didn't receive a letter, didn't hear from him, why hadn't she accepted the truth—that he wasn't coming back for her?

Tucker harped on her wonderful faith, but Ginny asked herself if it was faith or a blind insistence on getting her own way that had kept her in Jubilee Junction all this time. Maybe she hadn't been waiting on God. Maybe she'd simply refused to see that God wasn't going to give her the husband she craved and had made up her mind to circumvent His will.

On these thoughts followed the unthinkable. Perhaps she unwittingly added to Riley's misconceptions about their relationship, made him feel responsible for her, because she was afraid she'd never be married. He'd been willing to sacrifice everything for her. Was she so bent on her own way that she couldn't see the damage a relationship like that would have inflicted on her friend?

The questions plagued Ginny all the way home, all through the evening while she helped her father settle in, and into nighttime hours that should have been restful.

Finally Ginny knelt by her bed and turned it over to her heavenly Father.

I don't want to let go. I don't want to watch him walk away again. But staying here is not what Tucker wants. I'm tired of fixing things, God. All I do is make a worse mess. So I give it to You. Your will be done.

As she read the well-worn pages of her Bible into the

early morning hours, Ginny allowed the heavenly peace to wash over her and soothe her battered spirit.

Go or stay, whatever happened with Tucker now was out of her hands.

Chapter Eleven

Tucker heaved a sigh of relief as he flopped onto the grass and watched the members of Jubilee Junction's boy's group roast hot dogs.

Another club newspaper was ready to print, an eight-page edition this time. He saw Tom tease the others and reflected on the boy's relaxed attitude and lack of belligerence. In three short months the group had grown, expanded and solidified by tight bonds of camaraderie. And no one had changed more than Tom.

Tucker wasn't exactly sure how it had happened, but he was very grateful that it had. The boys still required direction and leadership, but each day saw them assume more and more responsibility for their lives. It was a big step on the road to their future.

Ginny sank down beside him.

"I'm very glad to be present at the launch party for this new expanded version of *Happenings*," she told him, beaming as if they were her own kids. "I love that name. It so completely captures what's going on with these guys."

"I'm glad you like it. Some people aren't quite so thrilled about our growing numbers or the things we're doing." He didn't tell her of the unexpected police checks that had been initiated by a member of town council.

"There's always one or two nonbelievers." She shrugged. "A couple more months with the guys in town and everyone will accept them as part of the landscape."

Tucker chuckled, his eyes on the assortment of unusual clothing and hair colors that appeared in the firelight.

"Maybe."

"Hey, Tuck, I've got an idea. I need some advice. Hi, Ginny." Tom flopped down beside them, his eyes glowing with suppressed excitement.

"Okay, Tom. I'll tell you what I can. Shoot."

"Well, it's like this. I know that I did some really awful things when I set those fires. I ruined people's lives and property and I feel real bad about it." He took a deep breath, then tugged two letters from his pocket. "So I thought maybe I could apologize for my actions. I don't know where some of them moved to, but I got two addresses from my probation officer. Will you read these and see if they're okay?"

Tucker took the letters reluctantly.

"I'll read them, if you want, but I'm sure that any apology you've made is just fine, Tom." He clasped the boy on the shoulder. "It's a pretty tough thing to do. I admire you for your courage."

"You do?" Tom stared, red hair glowing. "But you've done way harder things. I'm just following your example."

"M-my example?" What did the kid mean?

"Yeah." Admiration gleamed in the boy's eyes. "You had the courage to go to those places in the middle of wars, to take on a bunch of brats, the courage to let us figure out things for ourselves. I guess I can do this."

Ginny watched as the teenager nudged Tucker on the shoulder.

"You're like my guide, Tucker. I just try to follow what you do." He grinned. "Know what else? Marty showed me how to condense the spaces in the paper just a little. I'm going to put my apology in there, too. I want to make sure everyone knows I've changed. Then they won't have to worry so much and send police checks and stuff."

Tucker gulped, shifted uncomfortably under the spotlight of Tom's honesty. Thankfully Ginny's soft voice filled the gap.

"Good for you, Tom. I believe God will honor your decision to do the right thing."

"Yeah, I do, too. Thanks, Ginny." He grinned at her, then his attention flickered to Tucker. "You know how the preacher had those talks about all the things in our lives working together for good?"

"Uh, yeah. I guess so." Tucker didn't want to go into that—he didn't see the sense of it. His life certainly wasn't working out to anything good.

"Well, it took me a while to figure out exactly what he meant. I mean, how could my losing my family be good? How could getting in with the wrong bunch and setting fires work together to bring something good? Why would God even care about me?" Tom glanced around, his face serious.

Tucker wanted to protest, to tell him that he was a great kid. But Tom wasn't finished speaking.

"That's the funny thing, though, isn't it, Tucker? He does care. Look at these guys. Every one of us was on the edge, ready to fall over until you and Marty started this club and got us straightened out."

Straightened out? *He* hadn't done that! "Tom, I—"

"Because of you guys and the club, kids who didn't have a hope are learning better ways. That's the good that came out. Or some of it, anyway. That's what God's love does for us. If we let it."

Tucker had to stop this hero worship. It wasn't right. He didn't deserve it.

"I was a punk, you know that. A bratty punk who deserved to spend time in jail for what I did. God forgave me, but I had to forgive myself. It was hard at first. I didn't see why He let me get into that. But now I can sorta see some of the reason. All things really do work together for good."

Ira hailed him, brandishing a plain white platter loaded with chocolate squares. Tom jumped to his feet, all seriousness disappearing.

"Hey, Ginny, you didn't tell me you were bringing fudge for dessert!" He rushed off, anxious to get his share.

Tucker had to get away. He rose, dusted off his pants, then strode from the group into the cover of the trees. His hands clenched at his sides. Behind him, he heard Ginny's soft tread.

"If he only knew the truth about me, it would shatter those pretty illusions into nothing."

She shook her head. "I don't think so, Tucker. I think Tom would understand perfectly. He's made mistakes, he knows all about that. But Tom's also figured out what he needs to learn to make this experience count for something good."

A minute later she returned to the group with one of the boys who had volunteered to roast her a hot dog.

Tom's also figured out what he needs to learn to make this experience count for something good.

Tucker grimaced. If Tom could do it, why couldn't he? When no answer came, he walked to the fire, trying to shed the unanswered question.

"Okay, fellows. Tomorrow we'll print, then distribute our newest edition all over town. If you can get your chores done in time, we'll meet at the office, back door, at noon. We'll have all afternoon to sell them." Marty glanced around, his face shining with pride. "If we can sell enough, we'll finally be able to buy a motor for that plane. It's about time we got the thing into the air, don't you think?"

"Yeah!"

The resounding chorus made Tucker laugh. Anyone who saw their plane in the air would be certain it was a UFO, and not just because of the strange colors. He only hoped the lopsided wings would hold the body aloft. Not that it mattered. The boys were as proud of that airplane as they were of themselves for decorating it.

They jostled each other, each one teasing the other about his artwork. Ginny stood among them, eyes dancing with fun as she listened to the banter.

She would be a wonderful mother—loving, gentle, intuitive. She seemed to intrinsically know when to touch, when to praise, when to scold. She joined in the fun with no inhibitions, giving as good as she got. Why hadn't she been the one in charge of this group?

"Okay, guys. Sharing time. If you've finished stuffing your faces, let's gather round the fire." Marty took a seat and waited.

They took their places, bumping shoulder to shoulder on the logs arranged around the fire pit. Tucker reluctantly found a place at the end of one log.

He didn't like this part of their meetings. He always felt uncomfortable, vulnerable, when the kids started sharing personal stuff. It just seemed so—private. But Marty had insisted that the kids needed a place and time to open up, to spill whatever was bothering them.

"Tonight Tom's going to share a little bit of his life. Go ahead, Tom."

Tucker closed his eyes, wishing at that precise moment he were somewhere else. He'd grown close to this boy, felt a kinship with him. But he didn't want to know any more about his past, didn't want to open his heart any further. It was dangerous. And what good would it do? A year from now he'd be long gone. Getting so involved with this kid spelled trouble...because it would hurt.

The knowledge sucker-punched Tucker. He hadn't realized he was protecting himself. And from a kid, a homeless kid who'd made a couple of mistakes.

What kind of chickenhearted man was he?

"I grew up in a pretty rough situation."

Tucker's head jerked up in surprise.

"My mother had a boyfriend who lived with us, and he wasn't the best father you could have asked for. Us kids could never do anything right, no matter how hard we tried. I guess eventually I just quit trying."

Tucker glanced around the group, noticed the nods from several of the boys. Then he saw Ginny. Her eyes were riveted on Tom. Tears glistened in her eyes as she listened. Tucker gulped and looked away. He wouldn't let them get to him, either of them.

"I'm not blaming my dad for everything. We didn't

give him the respect we should have and we disobeyed my mom a lot. It wasn't exactly a happy home.''

In a lot of ways, Tom's childhood was like Tucker's. He'd never been able to appease his father, never measured up to the standard set by a man determined to lord it over his family.

''I suppose it was partly to get away that I started hanging around the streets at night. I didn't fit in anywhere, and when some guys asked me if I wanted to join them, I figured, why not? At least I'd have somebody.''

There, but for Adrian Brown and the grace of God, Tucker Townsend would have walked. He knew it as surely as he knew his name.

''They were just like me, alone, too much time on their hands. They'd already done a few nasty things and gotten away with it. If I wanted to be part of them, I had to prove myself. So I did. It started with burning a garbage can. They thought that was pretty cool, but they wanted more. So I gave it to them. I became the leader.'' He stopped, quelled the waver in his voice, then continued. ''When I was caught the third time, I'd set a fire in an apartment building. A little girl almost died.''

Stark silence greeted his words.

''I was at the bottom of the barrel, but I wouldn't admit it. I'd destroyed people's buildings, ruined their belongings, stolen their homes. Can you believe I thought I was the one who was the victim?'' He laughed at his foolishness. ''The judge said I couldn't stay in that neighborhood anymore. I was a threat. I got shuffled around until they sent me here. I was pretty mad and I figured if I did something bad enough, Marty would send me back.''

A noise in the trees behind Tucker disturbed him. He turned, searching for the cause, but saw nothing. An animal? He wasted a few more minutes examining the darkness as he continued to listen to Tom.

"I got kind of a surprise when I moved in with Marty."

They shared a glance of love that Tucker envied.

"Marty never gave up on me, didn't throw me out or call me names, he just loved me. That was a shocker." Tom grinned at his foster father. "I'm sure there were times when he could have strung me up, but he didn't. He just kept quietly teaching me about God, His love, His concern. And he kept saying God could work everything out."

Tucker gulped, fear clutching his stomach when Tom's gaze moved to him.

"I didn't really get that part of it. Not until Tucker came to town and the two of them started this group. Ginny and I were talking one day and she told me to look back in my life and trace the events in it up to this point." He nodded. "I did that. Then I mapped out what I knew of Tucker's life, and of Marty's, and I saw how God wove it all together into one big picture. Tucker got injured saving his friend and came back here because God needed to use him to help us."

No, Tucker wanted to yell. That isn't the truth. I didn't get injured saving my friend. I caused his death.

But no one was looking at him. All eyes were focused on Tom, a young boy who stood straight and tall before them, his gaze clear and steady as he told the truth.

"Anyway, all of this is just to say that everything in our lives happens for a reason. Once we understand that, we also understand that we're responsible for what we do in our lives. I'm going to talk to the people that I hurt, ask their forgiveness. If I can, I'll pay for my mistakes. And I'm going to work on being as good a man as Marty and Tucker are. We couldn't have better examples. Thank you both."

He walked to Marty, hugged him, eyes shining with joy. Tucker steeled himself, knowing his turn was next. His stomach roiled. His palms sweated. He had to tell the truth, to explain. He couldn't go on knowing Tom believed a lie. But how could he do that without losing their respect?

Sure enough, moments later Tom moved to stand in front of him, his face concerned.

"I know you've had a lot of grief, Tucker. I'm sorry for that. But God will use it, if you let Him." Then he stuck out a hand.

Tucker shook it, feeling the strength in his boyish grip.

"You're a good kid, Tom," he said quietly, a wash of humility rising inside him. "A very good kid."

Tom grinned. "If you like kids," he teased.

It was the perfect mood breaker. The other kids burst out laughing and teased each other. Tucker held on to Tom's hand. He had to say it.

"I'm glad you enjoyed the club, Tom. But please, don't think of me as a hero, because I'm not. I've done some things I'm not very proud of."

Tom smiled slowly. It was the kind of smile that wiggled its way from his lips to the dimples in his cheeks to the flash of joy in his eyes.

"Haven't we all?" he reminded. "The point is to learn from them. Marty says that's what wisdom is."

"He's a pretty smart kid, don't you think?" Ginny stood behind Tom, her face beaming into Tucker's. She leaned forward and brushed a kiss against Tom's cheek. "I'm so proud, I could dance."

"Not with me. Sorry. I don't dance. At all." Tom grinned. "You might talk Tucker into it, though." He lifted one eyebrow at Tucker, laughed and then raced away.

Ginny peered at him. "You're doing something good here, Tuck. Something very, very good."

"Yeah." For once Tucker ignored the guilt and enjoyed the moment. He looped his arm through Ginny's and led her toward the food table. "Did you save any of that fudge for me?" he whispered after spying the empty plate.

She slipped a foil-wrapped square out of her pocket. "One piece," she whispered, slipping it into his hand.

"You know—" he bit off a chunk and let it melt on his tongue "—it occurs to me that I should provide the food once in a while."

"You cook?" Her nose wrinkled up suspiciously.

He tilted his chin defiantly. "Of course I cook. Sort of. Actually, I was thinking of a restaurant meal."

"Well, you did buy me that chicken sandwich." She winked at him, her eyes bright, tender.

In that moment Tucker wanted nothing more than to bury himself in her arms and forget the rest of the world. Just to stay here, to spend evenings like this, would be heaven.

But he couldn't stay. He had a job to do. And sooner or later, he'd have to go back to it.

"I'm thinking maybe supper, tomorrow night. In your backyard." He waited a moment for her to catch his drift. "After I deliver all those papers, I'm going to need to work out the kinks."

"The hot pool." She caught on immediately. "Great. I'm quitting work at four. I've got someone coming in to help cover things till Dad's back in the harness."

"You promise you'll leave it all to me? You won't make dessert or a snack or anything?"

She peered at him, a hurt look in her eyes. "Well, I don't have to, if you'd rather I not," she began.

"I don't want you to do anything. From four o'clock on, you're a woman of leisure. I'll make sure your father has something to eat. Deal?"

She nodded slowly. "Okay. Deal."

As the group broke up and Ginny disappeared, Tucker asked himself why he'd made that date. Why let himself grow any more attached to her? The answer wasn't hard to find.

Because she'd done so much for the rest of them. Because she'd given and given, in spite of everything.

Because for once in his life, Tucker wanted to give something back, to feel like his life wasn't totally in the red.

Was that a good enough reason to risk getting her hopes up?

"This is the best suggestion you've had in years." Ginny laid her head against the rock and let the mineral-rich water soak her troubles away. "Even if it's closer to five than four. What took you so long?"

"Boy's club meeting. They're going through a list of possible candidates again. Six possibles." Tucker ducked his shoulders under the water, then sprawled on the other side of the pool, eyes closed as he, too, relaxed. "How are the house plans coming?"

"Very well. The foundation is laid, and they're starting the framework. It's going to be beautiful."

"Of course." He grinned. "You designed it."

His cell phone pealed a loud cry, disturbing the tranquillity of their soak. Tucker leaned over to pick it off the rocks where he'd placed it before entering the pool.

"Hello. Oh. Hi."

Ginny watched his face lose all color as he recognized the voice on the other end.

"Yeah. Okay. Not yet."

One hand gripped the edge of the stone basin, fingertips white as he listened.

"I can't tell you that. I'm not exactly sure, but I will let you know as soon as I am. Yeah. Thanks."

He clicked the phone shut and returned it to the rock, brown eyes wary as they met hers. He said nothing, simply sank into the water.

"Problems?" A frisson of trepidation wiggled down her spine at his glowering countenance.

"The network," he told her shortly. "They want to know when I'll be back. It's the second call this week."

"Oh." What could she answer to that? He didn't want her care or concern. He just wanted her to help heal his spirit. "Do you know when you're returning?"

He glared at her. "No."

"Oh."

She was about to change the subject when a piercing wail shattered the afternoon.

"The fire alarm?" Ginny scooted out of the pool, wrapped herself in a towel and headed toward the house, hearing Tucker's quick footsteps immediately behind her.

She hurried to the front of the house and stood on the step, trying to discover where the fire might be.

"I've got to go check the store," she told him. "That smoke is coming from the downtown area."

"I'll come with you. Maybe there's something I can do."

It took only seconds to pull on her jeans and a shirt. Tucker had to sprint back to the pool to collect his shoes, then they were off.

The closer they got to downtown, the better Ginny felt. The fire seemed to be at the other end of the street from the store. They rounded a corner, and she gasped.

"The paper!"

"I see it."

Flames licked out of windows where the glass had shattered, moving swiftly from one level to another. Ginny parked well back, out of the way, then caught up with Tucker, and they strode toward the building.

"Stay here, Ginny. I'm going to help."

Heart in her mouth, Ginny waited while he spoke to the policeman. A moment later he was back, face grim.

"Marty's gone inside," Tucker told her. "I've got to help."

Then he was gone. Ginny watched, praying fervently as one after another of the firemen were forced out of the burning building. The heat dried her skin, but she refused to back away. She had to be there when Tucker came out.

As she waited, she heard people behind her talking.

"They say a kid did it. Tall kid. Saw him running away, out the back of the building just before the fire was reported. Redheaded kid. Tom something."

Ginny whirled and glared at them, furious that anyone would start this kind of gossip.

"Well, don't look at me. I didn't identify him. Vera Malloy did that. Anyway, that kid's set fires before. He even said so in that newspaper they put out. Doesn't surprise me that he'd take it up here."

"It's a lie!" Ginny controlled her temper with difficulty. "Tom would never start a fire, especially not here. He loves this place."

"Yeah. Right. We know how much those punks love things."

A collective shout went up. Ginny turned to see Tucker, clad in a fireman's suit, emerge staggering from the fire. Marty's body lay slung over his shoulders, still and lifeless.

Helping hands relieved Tucker of his burden as he collapsed to the ground. Ginny rushed forward, side-stepping the police, grateful that the ambulance attendants were already caring for Marty.

"Please," she begged them. "I can help." Someone finally allowed her to pass the barricade.

"Tucker? Are you all right?" She eased off his hat and brushed a hand across his soot-darkened face. "Tucker?"

He coughed several times but eventually nodded. When he looked at her, she saw his eyes were streaming with tears.

"He was trying to save the boys' stuff," he said, voice scratched and gravelly. "He was worried about that stupid plane."

Ginny took the cup of water someone offered her and held it to his lips.

"Drink it," she ordered.

"Marty—"

"—is being taken of, Tucker. He's in good hands. Now drink."

He sipped a little, coughed, then sipped some more.

"Local hero does it again." The fire chief clapped him on the shoulder.

Tucker's soot-smeared face tightened. "Don't say that!"

Ginny had never heard his voice so fierce or so angry. The fireman backed up, hands in the air.

"Hey, all I was saying was thanks. We needed an extra hand down there. All that paper makes it pretty tough to control a blaze like this. You were in the right place at the right time."

"Yeah, well, it was no big deal. Okay?"

"Sure." The fire chief glanced at the building. "It's under control now. Just a matter of putting out spot fires. There's a lot of damage, though."

"I know." Once he'd caught his breath, Tucker stood, glancing around for the ambulance.

"They took him away already," the fireman explained in solemn tones. "He's in rough shape."

"How rough?"

"A guess?" The chief scratched his head. "I'd say at least second-degree burns on his hands and arms. Maybe third on his back. But you can never be sure. Sometimes it looks worse than it is." He waved a quick farewell, then moved to direct his team.

"It's those kids, that's what it is. Why, if we'd never had that bunch of hooligans in our town, they wouldn't have started Marty's paper on fire."

Tucker froze, his face blanching as the conversation behind them resumed.

"That little arsonist. That's the one that did it. Vera even saw him running out the back."

Ginny shook her head. "They don't know that, Tucker," she said. "It's just gossip."

But the crowd decried her.

"Vera saw him. Who else has hair like that? Orange as a carrot."

"Tom." Tucker's shoulders slumped. He closed his eyes as he whispered the name. "They're accusing Tom."

"He didn't do it," Ginny insisted.

"Well, of course he didn't!" Tucker opened his eyes and glared at her. "But how are we going to prove it?" He glanced around as if he could find a clue.

Ginny knew what he was looking for. She glimpsed some of the boys standing away from the rest of the spectators. She touched Tucker's arm. "There."

Tucker nodded, shuffled to his feet, then started walking toward them, eyes searching the group for Tom. Ginny already knew he wasn't there.

"You guys know where Tom is?"

They shook their heads, faces sober.

"Any ideas?"

"He was going to take papers out to the farms on the old Willing's Road. Thought he could sell a few extras, I guess. But he should have been back by now." Nick spoke for the rest of the group. "Is it bad?"

"Really bad. Marty's gone to the hospital."

Ginny knew he was going to tell them, and she wanted to stop it. With every fiber of her being she longed for him to keep silent. But it wouldn't help. They would hear soon enough what everyone was saying. They would know half the town suspected them— or one of them—of lighting this fire. Better to hear it from Tucker.

"Someone claims they saw Tom run out of the back of the building right before the alarm was heard. You guys know anything, you'd better tell me now."

"Tom?" Without hesitation Nick shook his head. "No way."

"He left right after the meeting." Ira kicked a clod

of dirt. "He wouldn't have done it, Tucker. He loved this club."

"I know. I don't believe it. I'm just trying to sort everything out. John, I want you and Ira to round everybody up and meet at Ginny's, by the clubhouse. We've got to think this through."

They nodded, then hurried away, shocked by the events. Ginny looked at Tucker.

"What are you going to do?" she whispered.

"I'm going to prove Tom had nothing to do with this. But first, I'm going to find out how bad the fire was. Are you coming?"

"Try and stop me." Without thinking she threaded her fingers into his and matched his step across the street.

She stood silent while he questioned the chief, fully aware of the accusing glare of the townspeople. Finally she spotted her father's thin figure near the back. Mrs. Franks stood beside him, holding his arm.

"I'll be back in a minute, Tucker," she whispered, then eased her hand away. He glanced at her once, then his attention was back on the chief.

"Hi, honey."

"Oh, Daddy." She hugged him close for several moments, savoring the warmth of his embrace. "They're saying Tom did it, Dad. Marty's in the hospital. He's in trouble. Can you find the pastor and get him to start the prayer chain? We really need it now."

"That boy wouldn't hurt a flea. Ridiculous bunch of busybodies!" Her father bristled, his eyes flashing. "I'll start recruiting right here. Half the church is standing beside me, anyway. They might as well put their tongues to better use."

Ginny had to suppress a smile as her father approached first one bystander, then another, asking if they'd be willing to help. Grateful that he knew how to deal with each of them, she hurried to Tucker.

"I see. So possibly by Monday I could go in and see what to make of things?" He nodded. "Okay. In the meantime, can you let me know if you find anything? *Anything?*"

"Sure."

They turned away. Tucker went first, parting the crowd so they could get through. They were walking toward her car when Ginny spotted Tom riding his bike into town.

"Tucker, look!"

As they watched, he pedaled at an even speed. But then he caught sight of the smoke and began to pedal increasingly faster.

Tucker waved to him, and the boy skidded to a halt beside them.

"What happened?" Tom stared at the newspaper building, then at them. "What's wrong?"

"Where have you been?"

"I rode out to deliver some papers. I earned an extra fifteen dollars, enough to buy us that motor Marty talked about." He held out the money proudly.

Tucker took it, his face grim as he spoke.

"There was a fire at the paper, Tom. I'm not sure the plane even survived."

Tom gasped, then his face went completely white.

"Marty was going to go over some stuff for next week's edition," he sputtered, eyes tearing up. "He was working inside. I have to go help him." He dropped the bike, ready to charge to the rescue.

Tucker reached out a hand to stop him, his face as ashen as the boy's.

"Marty's at the hospital. He's been injured. No one knows how badly yet." He stopped for a minute as if unsure how to continue. "Tom, someone claims they saw you leaving the building just before the fire started."

"What?" Tom frowned. "But I wasn't even in town!"

"I know. But the allegation is there. Can you identify your time at all? Maybe think of someone who would remember seeing you?"

As the full import of what Tucker was asking sunk in, Ginny saw the boy's countenance fall.

"But I didn't do it! You believe me, don't you, Tucker?"

"Yes, of course I believe you. Ginny does, too." Tucker drew her into the circle. "We know you would never have started that fire, but it would be an idea to get some proof out there before the accusations get going."

"It sounds like they already are." Tom kicked the dust with his toe. Then he looked at Tucker, trust implicit in his eyes. "I didn't do it. Can't we go and see Marty now?"

"Yeah, we can." But Tucker stood where he was. "We'll go and see him right away. But first I want you to think. Can anybody place you at their house at a time that would make it impossible for you to have come back here and start that fire?"

Tom, his eyes fixed on Tucker, solemnly shook his head. "No."

"Why not?"

"I didn't come straight back," Tom admitted. "I went to the falls."

"Tom!" Ginny couldn't believe it. "You know how dangerous it is."

"I didn't go near them. I just wanted to look along the bank. I heard some men in town talking about fossils they'd found, and I wanted to see if I could find any. Marty likes to collect them."

Tucker sighed, closed his eyes and thought. Ginny felt sorry for him. Tom was his protégé, the boy's group his special outreach. Even if he didn't realize it, she knew the talk would run rampant through the town. The boys, particularly Tom, would be targeted as mischief makers. Being accused of starting this fire might invalidate Tom's probation.

"We've got to think of something to clear you. We've got to."

Tom's face shone, his eyes brimming with joy. "I'm glad you believe me, Tucker," he admitted quietly. "It isn't much of an alibi, but God knows I didn't set that fire. He'll work things out. All things work together for good."

Tucker blinked at such blind assurance, and in that moment Ginny knew what was going through his mind. Tucker didn't have the same level of faith, wasn't prepared to stand by and let God work it out. Instead, Tucker wanted to make sure of the boy's defense before it was needed.

Now Tom was the comforter, patting Tucker's shoulder to encourage him.

"Now I'd like to see Marty. I want to make sure he knows I didn't do this."

"Don't worry, Tom. Marty knows." Ginny wrapped her arm around the boy's thin shoulders and hugged him. "But, yes, I think we should go over to the hospital and see what's happening."

As they drove, Ginny felt a sense of grim foreboding hanging like thick smoke.

What would happen to the boy's group? And how would Tucker react to yet another tragedy? What if Marty died?

God had initiated another test of patience. There was nothing she could do but wait and see.

Chapter Twelve

"I'm sorry, Mr. Townsend. It's admirable that you're trying to help Mr. Owens by keeping his weekly editions running. We appreciate the work you and your, er, group of boys have done to get the offices up and functioning. But we must tell you that we have grave doubts about keeping this group going."

Tucker almost groaned as the mayor looked to his council for agreement. To a man, they nodded. Two weeks later and they were more convinced than ever that Tom was the culprit.

"The fire chief has determined the fire resulted from a match in the basement. Your boys met there frequently. It's hard to justify continuing support for this group when so much damage has resulted."

"No one has proven that *any* member of the boy's group was in any way involved." Tucker bristled at the unfairness of it. Ginny's fingers crept around his under the table, infusing him with courage. He tried to soften his words. "I don't believe it's a good thing to condemn anyone without evidence."

"Tucker, there was an eyewitness." Rob Lassiter frowned. "I'm new to council, but that's pretty tough evidence to refute."

"Plus the boy himself admitted that he set fires." The mayor tilted his chair. "He told us his record the very day of the fire. Right in that newspaper of theirs."

"Yes, because he wants to make restitution! Those are not the actions of a person who's planning to commit new crimes."

It was a waste of time, he could see that just by looking at their faces. They'd made up their minds and weren't prepared to adjust their decision without some cold, hard evidence to the contrary.

"But you do agree that the group may continue?" Ginny leaned forward to address them. "You aren't going to cancel your agreements with the agencies concerned? The funding you promised will remain in place?"

The mayor glanced from one member to the other. When he spoke, his voice was cool.

"For now the agreements stand. These partnerships have brought needed income for projects we wouldn't otherwise be able to consider. The youth center is one of those Jubilee Junction children could benefit from as well as—er, others. We don't want to sever any connections until we're in possession of all the facts."

"In other words, they're not ready to kiss off the money, even if they want the kids gone," Tucker muttered under his breath.

Ginny tossed Tucker a look that told him to keep his lips sealed.

"Thank you, Mayor. I'm sure the truth will out and the entire town will realize that Tom is not to blame for this fire."

The mayor nodded. "Now, if you'll excuse us, we will be behind closed doors for the rest of this session."

Tucker followed Ginny from the room, indignation boiling as they walked out of the town hall and down the street side by side.

"At least they haven't forbidden you to continue." She tried to sound cheerful. "That's something."

"Not much. Anyway, I'm not sure they could stop a private citizen from running a group."

"Maybe not. But they could stop the funding, and that would hurt everybody in town. We've got to figure something out."

"I wish I'd never gotten involved in this," Tucker muttered. "I let you talk me into thinking I could do some good, help out. I should have known it would fall apart." He felt the boiling anger return. "Marty's doctor thinks he's going to have to retire. His lungs aren't in good condition. But without the paper to support him, he's lost most of his income."

"But I thought you said that nephew of his is going to help out. Surely he'll keep things running until Marty sells out?"

"If he sells out. Who'd want to buy a paper in the condition that one is?" Despair waited in the darkness, ready to overwhelm him. "Why did I do this? I pushed and pushed, I told them they could be anything, do anything, go anywhere. I let them think the past was behind them, that it had nothing to do with the future they chose. What a lie!"

"Stop it!" Ginny planted herself in front of him, her nose an inch from his chest. "It wasn't a lie. They deserve the chance to dream as much as anyone." She satisfied herself with one last glare, then marched forward, her purple leather shoes slapping against the cement with a loud clatter.

"Of course they do." Tucker matched his step to hers. He raked a hand through his hair. "It's just—I wish I hadn't offered them such a big carrot, demanded so much. If the group has to fold, it's going to be a major disappointment." He stopped in front of her house.

"I thought maybe I could help change things, make up for—before. You know? I figured I could clear my conscience by proving I'm not a total washup as a human being."

"Tucker—"

He shook his head.

"But I haven't. I've only made things worse." He looked at her. "Sorry, Ginny."

She shook her head. "Don't you apologize to me, Tucker Townsend. You go apologize to those boys, tell them you're giving up on them, that you made a mistake, took a chance that didn't work out the way you wanted." She took a step closer. "Go ahead. I dare you."

Tucker stared. She was furious. At him!

"You go to that meeting tomorrow night and you tell them that you're sorry you tried to change their lives. You quit on them, and then you stand there and watch the life drain out of their eyes." She slapped her hands on her hips, her eyes flashing emerald fire.

"Gin, I—"

"Then, after you've done that, you go sit in the corner and sulk about your bad luck, your nasty life, the hard decisions you've had to make. You do that while everyone else picks up the pieces. It's an old pattern, isn't it, Tuck? Familiar, easy. Comfortable.''

Ginny, I—''

''I'll survive, Tucker. So will they.'' She squinted at him, her eyes losing some of their fire.

Sadness crept over her face, dimming the vibrancy he'd always admired. Her voice whispered to him in the stillness.

''But will you, Tucker? Will you walk away and forget us all? Will seven years from now find you sitting in Siberia some lonely night, after you've covered another headline story, wondering if Tom ever went to college? If Nick did something with that genius he has for motors? If John got over his allergies?''

She opened the gate, stepped through, then turned, her face in shadow. He didn't need to see it to know that her mouth drooped in a sad little smile, that her eyes were filling with tears, that her gorgeous hair hung dark and heavy against her back. He didn't need to see it to know the hope was draining out of her.

''You want pat answers to tough questions, Tucker. You want me to tell you why.'' She hiccuped a sob.

He could feel the rigid control she exerted as she spoke. He forced himself to listen, though he hated every word.

''Well, I don't know why. I only know that this is a chance for you to overcome the difficulties you've faced, to take on the challenge you've been given and prove to yourself that God is here, waiting for you. Prove that He has given you enough strength, enough brains and enough of everything you need to do whatever He asks. You want answers from God? Ask Him. There will never be a better opportunity.''

She turned and walked up the path, then let herself into the house without saying good-night. Tucker waited, watched as lights flickered on, then off. After a while the house was dark.

Her words repeated over and over, like a recording that would not be silenced.

Opportunity. Opportunity.

He needed to think, to sort everything out, get his mind cleared.

Tucker went where he'd always gone to think. He slipped in through the Browns' back gate and strode down to the water. The old maple was still there, big and welcoming, its branches splayed just enough to cuddle him in its embrace.

The moon shone bright and round, illuminating the tree house in a silver wash. Would they ever use that tree house again? Would they push and shove their way into the hot pool he and Ginny had enjoyed so often in the past? Would anyone be around to encourage the boys to ignore obstacles and press on?

The past rolled over him in a tidal wave of memories that he couldn't squelch. Tucker didn't even try. Finally he faced it all.

"I'm sick of running away, sick of feeling guilty and sick of never knowing. If You're there, please help me. Show me the truth, God. Set me free."

He wasn't going to go down without a fight. Not this time. He'd started something here, something good. Just because he hit a glitch didn't mean he would run away like a scared rabbit. Tucker Townsend was done with running away.

Marty was his friend. Tom looked up to him. The rest of the group depended on him, took their cues from his decisions.

Tucker stared into the sky. Ginny claimed that God was there, waiting to help him, to show him.

"I'm not giving up," he whispered. "Maybe I'm not the hero Tom thinks I am, but I'm not a quitter, either. The station will want me back. I haven't got a lot of time." He took a deep breath and spoke the words that committed him to seeing this thing through.

"There's got to be some clue to prove Tom didn't do it, right, God? Help me find it? Please?"

"Tucker? Tucker, what are you doing up there?"

Ginny's voice penetrated the mist of sleep as it had so many mornings in their childhood. Lost in a dream of the past, Tucker debated. Was it past or present?

He opened his eyes and grinned. Present, definitely present, he told himself as he caught a glimpse of her panda-bear slippers. Those were not the ankles of a child.

"Have you been here all night?"

He eased himself out of his perch, rubbing his neck as he did. "Yeah, I guess."

"You idiot! You could have fallen and broken your neck and no one would have known." Her pink fuzzy robe flapped in the breeze that ruffled her curls into a frothy mess.

He watched her lips part at the exact moment his cell phone rang.

"Hold that thought, Gin." Tucker fished out the phone and flipped it open. "Hello? Hi." It was *them* again. He listened, all pleasure in the day draining away as the words washed over him.

"Who? When?" He swallowed. "You're sure it's Ulysses? I see. No, he's not bluffing. Yes, I'll come. Let me know when."

He clipped the phone closed without thinking, the fear rising like a phantom. Why now?

"Tucker? What's wrong?"

He stared at her for a moment, wondering why she was there.

"That was the network. They sent someone to take my place, to cover my story. He's a rookie, doesn't know diddly about Africa. He's been captured by a militia group."

"Ulysses's militia group."

She'd heard enough, Tucker noticed. He told her the rest.

"That bunch don't let people wander through their territory. Particularly not since they tried it last year and got some very negative press. They've had an uphill battle to prove they're not hooligans ever since."

"What aren't you saying, Tucker?" She sat on a nearby rock and drew her robe around her legs.

"They'll give him up if I go and talk to them, do a story that shows their side of the conflict. If I don't go, they've threatened to kill my replacement." He lifted his eyes to meet hers, let her see the fear crowding him. "It's my fault he's there, Gin. He went to do my job. I have to go."

"Yes, you do." Her voice was steady, calm, relieved.

"I'm scared." It was the first and only time he'd ever said those words aloud. But they were the truth, and Tucker was determined to deal only in truth from this point on.

"I know." She smiled a funny, understanding grin.

"I've made a big mess of things, Gin. You were right, I was feeling sorry for myself. And by doing that, I avoided responsibility. I pretended I was responsible, but what I really wanted was someone to come and make it all go away.'' He shrugged. ''I guess this means it isn't going away.''

''No.''

The silence that yawned between them wasn't awkward or strange. He sensed that she deliberately kept silent so he could marshal his thoughts.

''It's time for me to go back there and face the fear, Gin. Time to let God be in charge. It's time I tested what I've learned here, from you.'' He moved to crouch in front of her. ''I've learned so much, Ginny. You've given me so many things, so much patient understanding. Last night I asked God to tell me why the things that happened had to happen at all. I guess now He's going to show me.''

She smiled, tears shining in her eyes.

''But I don't want to go until I tell you something. If I'm going to be dealing with the truth, I need to tell you the truth. It might hurt, but it's the truth.''

''Truth is good.'' She sat there, waiting.

Tucker took her hands in his, held them tightly and began.

''All of my life I felt like second best, felt that I had to prove I could do things, could be good at something. We lived next door to you, and I saw how great your home was.'' He tried to smile and failed. ''Mine wasn't like that, Gin. My family was about as far from the perfect Christian home as you can imagine. And I was about as far from a Christian as it's possible for anyone to be.''

''Tucker, you don't have—''

He stopped her, one finger against her lips.

''Yes,'' he told her firmly. ''I do. So let me.''

She studied him for several moments, then nodded.

''I felt like a failure and I had proof whenever I compared myself and my family to yours. I guess that's why

I never had your assurance that God was there for me."
He sighed. "Then came college."

Her face lost its joyful look, so Tucker hurried with
this part.

"I did love you, Ginny. And I was going to return
and marry you. I always meant to keep our pact and to
keep my promise. Don't ever doubt that."

"Okay." She smiled.

"I made up my mind what I wanted to do, but my
family didn't agree. They didn't believe in my dream.
I was determined to prove them wrong. That's why I
didn't stay behind when you did. I was afraid I wouldn't
follow through, and I had to. I had to, Ginny."

I know." She nodded. Tears rolled down her cheeks.

Tucker made himself concentrate on what he was
saying, on getting it right.

"So I started college, and that first year I won a
scholarship. That was like vindication for me. It was
my chance to prove to my family, the town, myself,
that I was worthy of this. That I could make it. Then I
found out why my parents had to move from Jubilee
Junction so quickly. They were getting a divorce, and
they didn't want their fellow parishioners to know. Failure again."

He shrugged.

"I'm sorry, Tuck." Ginny brushed his arm with her
hand. "Very sorry."

"I had to make it in school. I couldn't possibly come
back here for you until I'd proven myself to you, your
father, the town. I had to be worthy of you."

"You always were," she whispered, one finger trac-
ing the curve of his jaw. "You didn't need college or
anything else to prove that."

He kissed the palm of her hand, then cradled it in his.

"I studied every chance I got, worked two jobs, took extra classes through the summer. I pushed as hard as I could. One day someone noticed, and I got a chance to work with a master. It was a godsend I couldn't ignore."

Now came the hard part. Tucker sucked in a breath of courage.

"I knew I could do it. I knew if I just kept my eyes on the goal, I would make it. I told myself that if I came back here, visited you, let my concentration lapse for a second, I'd lose my determination and never fulfill my dream. I'd be a failure." He swallowed, allowing the truth to emerge. "I couldn't take that chance, so I decided it would be easier if I didn't contact you at all."

The grief on her face burned straight to his heart.

"I'm sorry, Ginny. Truly. I knew it would hurt you, but I didn't see any other way. I rationalized my decision, told myself you'd be glad when you realized what I'd accomplished."

"But you never came back." She glanced at him, tears shimmering on the ends of her lashes.

"I know."

"Why, Tucker?" She smiled through her tears. "Funny, isn't it? This time I'm the one asking why."

"I don't know if I can explain this properly. I'm not even sure I completely understand it."

"Try."

He sighed. He owed her that—an explanation—at the very least. She'd waited, hoped, kept the faith. He'd left her high and dry.

"I was offered a job by my mentor. It was my chance. If I could prove myself, he promised I'd have more opportunities than I'd ever imagined. In the back of my mind I heard my dad and his words all over again. This was a fluke. I would never make it as a reporter. You and I wouldn't make it. Not unless we had something to build on. Something other than love."

"But—"

"I watched them mess up their lives, Ginny. All in the name of love. They divorced each other, married someone else and divorced them, too. My sister left her husband after ten years because she didn't love him any more. She found someone new."

"I'm sorry." She reached out to touch him, then let her hand drop to her lap.

"I know. So was I. But the message was sinking in, and the more stories I covered, the more I saw the truth of it. Love didn't matter one whit when greed and lust took over. What we'd had in high school—it wouldn't have lasted. It was just a kid thing, a fairy tale we dreamed existed. After a while I believed what I told myself. So I never came home, never had the courage to find out the truth."

He turned away, not wanting Ginny to see how much this hurt.

"Then Quint died. There, in the middle of that nightmare, with shots whizzing past me left and right, I realized that I was no different than anyone else." He dashed the moisture from his eyes, furiously angry with himself for denying the truth for so long.

The sun crawled across the sky with pink flamingo fingers that bathed the wooded glen in dawn. Tucker noticed, but kept his attention on the issue at hand.

"My need for fame, that craving to prove I was more than just the son of a loser—all of that and more superceded my watching out for the one person who'd stuck to me no matter what.'' He swallowed. ''I sacrificed Quint for my own greed, just like my dad sacrificed our entire family for some younger, prettier woman.''

There. He'd said it. Admitted the truth, shredded the lies and the pretense that he'd clung to for so long.

''I'm the author of my own problems, Ginny. I did it to myself. And to you. I'm sorry.''

''It's okay, Tuck. I forgave you a long time ago.'' She drew his face around so she could look into his eyes. ''We often create our own unhappiness. It's called being human.''

Now that he'd said it, he wanted all of it out. The truth laid bare to heal in the fresh, warm sunlight of day. Then he'd take the next step.

''I only proposed to Amanda because I had some stupid idea that marriage would solve my problems.''

''But no one else can make us happy, can they? It has to come from inside.'' She nodded, her face gentle, caring. ''Sometimes that's the hardest thing to accept. I'm glad you told me, Tucker.''

''But do you know why I did decide to tell you the truth?'' He hardened himself for the ordeal ahead.

Ginny's eyes opened wide. She lifted her shoulders. ''You needed to talk?''

''Maybe. But that wasn't all of it. I wanted to explain why I can't resume our relationship, why I can't just pick up where we left off.''

''Oh.''

It was like watching the sun go behind a cloud. The joy drained out of her face, left her eyes wary, watchful.

''I don't believe in happily ever after, Gin. It's a myth, a fairy tale. I have to deal in truth.''

''And the truth is that you don't love me. Am I

right?'' She lifted her chin. ''That's what you mean, isn't it?''

''I care about you, Ginny. You're the warmest, most loving person I've ever known. You've got a special place in my life, and if I was ever to marry anyone, it would be you.''

''But?''

''But love—'' He shook his head. ''It's something I can't understand, Gin. Something I can't quite get a handle on. It seems fickle to me. You fall in and you fall out. My father's fallen in love four times since he left my mother. I don't want to be like that.''

''Why, Tucker? Why not?'' She studied him intently, leaning slightly forward on her perch.

He thought for a moment. Why was love so dangerous? Why, God? What made him fear taking such a risk?

''Because I'll fail. I'll be a failure. Again.''

She grinned.

Tucker stared at her in puzzled disbelief. She was grinning like a cat who'd found canary on the menu.

A minute later her arms were wrapped tightly around him, her cheek pressed to his.

''Oh, Tucker, sometimes I just want to slap you!''

''Really?'' Just for a minute he let his arms circle her waist, felt her warmth press against him, her heart thud into his chest. Just for a minute he closed his eyes and reveled in the sensation.

''Yes, I do.'' She leaned back far enough to stare into his face. ''You are not a failure. Not now, not then. Not ever. You've achieved wonderful things, but the best thing is you've let in the light.''

''I have?'' He couldn't help asking the question. He didn't understand anything she was saying. But as long as Ginny Brown stood in the circle of his arms, he wasn't sure he cared.

"Yes, you have. Now go the rest of the way, Tuck. Hand it all over to God and see what He'll make out of it. Let go and trust, Tucker. If you can't trust anyone else, trust God."

Then she stood on her fluffy tiptoes and kissed him as if he were someone infinitely precious to her.

Tucker kissed her back. He was in the desert, had been for months, and she was an oasis. He clung to her like a lifeline. He'd expected recriminations, anger, tears. But not this. Never this. He'd never expected that Ginny Brown would let him be in her world on his terms.

"I love you, Tucker Townsend. I love you more than I ever dreamed, more than I imagined, more than life itself. You're buried here—" one hand touched her chest "—deep inside my heart. I will always love you. It doesn't matter where you go, what you do or when you come back, that place is reserved for you."

A pain stabbed him, an ache. He couldn't tell her the same thing. He couldn't give her the one thing she wanted from him.

"You've never failed me, Tucker. Not once. I've always believed in you, always trusted you. That's what love is. And whether you love me back or not doesn't change a thing."

"I care about you, Ginny."

"I know." She smiled, pressing a lock of hair off his forehead. "You tell me that every day."

"I do?" He frowned. "It's not love. It's just—caring."

She nodded, eyes shining. "I know."

He let his arms drop to his sides, wondering how to keep her from getting her hopes up.

"I have to go back there, Gin. I can't get out of it even if I wanted to. It's a test I have to get through. I don't know what will come of it, but I feel like everything has been leading up to this particular moment."

Ginny nodded. "A test of trust," she whispered, face glowing in the sun. "You'll pass, Tucker. And when you come back, I'll be right here. Still loving you."

"I don't want you to wait, Gin. I don't know how long this will take. Or even if I'll come back."

"I'll be here."

"You deserve to be happy."

"I am very happy."

"I don't want you to get your hopes up," he blurted out at last, frustrated by his inability to make her see that he wasn't offering love.

She smiled so wide, Tucker stared. Pure joy radiated around her in the dewy morning, kissing her skin with an iridescence that made her more beautiful than he remembered.

"That's the thing about happily ever after, Tucker. What it really means is hope. Hope for a future that's blessed with love and joy and contentment. I will have my happily ever after, Tucker. So will you."

He couldn't let her go. Not like this. Not waiting another seven years.

Tucker leaned down and kissed her again.

"I'll make you a promise," he whispered, brushing his thumb against the rose-petal softness of her cheek. "If I come back in one piece, in my right mind, I'll marry you."

She froze, her eyes searched his, plunging to the very depths of his soul in their quest for honesty.

"Do you mean it?"

He nodded.

"I mean it. I don't know what love is, Ginny. Or what it means. But I do know that there isn't anyone else I'd rather be married to than you. We've had this—this bond for seven years. Maybe it can last. I'm willing to give it a shot. When I come back."

She winked, an impish glow lighting her eyes.

"This bond is going to last a lot longer than that, Tuck. You'd better prepare yourself for a lifetime of love."

Her father's voice penetrated the stillness of the morning.

"Oh, my goodness, I've got to go. Dad'll be wondering where breakfast is." She tilted on her toes and brushed a kiss against his chin. "When will you leave?"

He shrugged. "All they said is to be ready. I'm going to get the boys together tonight. I don't like to just run out on them with things so upset." He dared to let himself touch her tousled curls. "Will you be there?"

"Try and stop me." She put her hand over his, holding it. "All things work together for good," she reminded him. "Hang on to that happily-ever-after verse."

"I'll try." He stared into her lovely face and felt a rush of peace. He'd done his best, told the truth as he understood it. "Now it's up to God," he murmured.

"Who better?" She grinned sassily, hugged him, then took off to the house, fuzzy slippers slapping against the grass.

Tucker followed more slowly, pausing to wave at Adrian.

Okay, Lord. If you sent me to Jubilee Junction in

order to leave again, I'm finally ready. My trust is in You.

He headed for Coach's house and his suitcase. Time for phase two in this trust business.

Chapter Thirteen

"I'm sorry, guys."

A collective groan went up from the seventeen boys gathered in the Browns' backyard. Tucker waved them down.

"I thought we'd have one last evening together, but I've been ordered to leave in less than an hour. I guess God has other plans for us." Tucker tried to smile, but he felt his spirit stalling at the challenges ahead. "I'd like you guys to promise me something."

They nodded. "Sure, man. Yeah."

"Tom is innocent. We all know that."

Loud cheers greeted this statement. Tom sat with the others, his face a mixture of sadness and pride in the faith of his comrades.

"I intended to look for a way to prove that, but I can't." Tucker walked over and held out a hand to Tom. "So I want you guys to do it."

The boy rose, took the outstretched hand and shook it firmly.

"My faith is in you, Tom. You've made a believer

out of me. All things work together, you told me. Well, I'm convinced. You're going to work this out, too. I can hardly wait to hear how you're going to use your life."

"Thanks, Tucker. I'll be praying for you, too. All things work together." He grinned.

Silence fell on the little group as Adrian Brown led a man dressed in military uniform onto the deck.

"Tucker, I believe your ride is here."

Tucker nodded. "Thanks. I'll be right there." Then he turned to the boys. "You guys keep the faith. Do what you can to help at the paper, stay out of trouble and keep that curfew. I don't know when I'll be back, but when I am, I'll expect to hear everything. Okay?"

"Yes, sir."

He waved, saluted, then walked onto the deck.

He, Adrian and Ginny followed the officer through the gate to the front of the house. A plain black sedan sat parked at the curb.

"I'll say goodbye here," Adrian murmured. He stretched out a hand. "I'm very proud of you, son. I'd like to hear all about it when you return."

Tucker nodded, too moved to say anything. He shook Adrian's hand. Adrian studied his face, nodded and walked away.

Ginny's hand slipped into Tucker's. She was openly weeping. He whispered a prayer for courage.

"Could you give us a moment?" he asked the sergeant.

The man nodded and walked to the car. Tucker led Ginny to a shadowed place under the maple tree where they'd shared their first kiss.

"Don't cry, Gin." He wiped away her tears.

"I can't help it. I'm scared."

He smiled, shook his head. "You? Afraid? Gimme a break, Gin. You've got the faith of ten warriors. You know whose hands I'm in."

"I know, but—"

He touched her lips in the barest skim of a kiss.

"I came back here because of your faith. I made it through one of the worst times in my life because you had faith. Don't stop trusting now."

"Okay." She sniffed, then wiped her eyes with the backs of her hands just as she had when they were eight and she'd fallen off his bike.

"Here. These are for you." He lifted the sheaf of pale yellow roses from their hiding place. "They're supposed to represent gold, a symbol of my promise to come back."

"Tucker, they're lovely!" She buried her face in the velvet petals. "Thank you."

He didn't need thanks. Watching her was enough.

"I wanted to give you something to solidify my promise, something tangible that you can hang on to until I get back. Actually I wanted to get you a diamond ring, but I didn't have time." He pulled his college ring off his finger. "Will this do?"

She stared at it, then at him, her eyes wide and deeply green.

"Tucker, are you sure?"

He nodded.

"It's the one thing I am sure of, Ginny Brown. I'm coming back. And if you're still willing, we're going to get married. I don't know anything about love, but maybe I can learn. You know enough to teach me."

He pushed the ring onto her finger, staring at it in the soft evening light.

"This is my promise, Gin. I'll be back."

"I love you, Tucker."

She melted into his arms for a kiss that shook him to his foundations.

When he finally lifted his head, her eyes were shining, all doubts erased.

"I'll be waiting, Tuck. And when you get back, I'm going to show you happily ever after."

He nodded. She'd laid her heart bare for him, held nothing back. He was scared, so scared that he would hurt her by never learning to love.

"Can you do one thing for me while you wait? Could you try and find something to help Tom?"

She nodded. "Of course."

"The fire chief said something about matches being found at the scene. But when I was talking to Tom about his past, he mentioned that he'd always used a lighter. I have a hunch that's a clue, but I just can't connect it up."

"Don't worry, Tuck. We'll figure it out. Tom's not going to jail."

He had to go. There was a plane waiting for him at some undisclosed location. The military had become involved, and everything was top secret.

And yet he lingered, his eyes memorizing every detail of Ginny Brown, his mind imprinting the scent of her, the smile, the brave quiver at the corner of her lips that she couldn't quite hide.

"Go with God, Tucker."

"Keep the faith, Gin. For me." He kissed her once more. "I will be back. I promise. Don't you forget it."

She grinned, pinched his arm. "As if!"

He laughed. For the first time in years joy bubbled inside him and broke free. She'd done that for him.

"Bye, Gin." He moved toward the car. The door

opened. Tucker set one foot inside, then turned to her. "I like the shoes," he murmured.

She froze for one long moment, then glanced at her bare feet. He knew she was laughing through the tears that trickled down her cheeks.

"Buy a new pair for my homecoming," he told her softly. "Something really special."

"You've got it." She winked, then waved.

Tucker got in the car and sat silent as it drove away. At the last minute he turned. She was still standing there. As if she knew he watched, she lifted her hand in a wave.

"Goodbye, Gin," he whispered and wondered if he'd ever see her again.

He hoped so. Suddenly it was very important that he come back to Ginny Brown. Suddenly Tucker had something very important to say.

"But you can't!" Ginny stared at the assembled council, aghast at their decision. "You can't cancel the deal. The boys are doing so well. It's summer! We'd planned a bunch of programs."

"I'm sorry, Ginny, you'll just have to unplan them. We simply can't allow the group to continue. In the absence of proof to the contrary, we're going to have to assume that boy was responsible."

"His name is Tom," she said, teeth clenched to stop the words she longed to utter. "And he has not been *convicted* of anything."

"The decision is final."

Though she saw compassion in many eyes, Ginny knew the case was lost. She'd tried everything she could think of, pulled every string she knew. But Marty's injuries combined with the constant reminder of the burned building kept the fear burning brightly in the Junction.

She rose to her feet, Tucker's ring burning a spot on her finger.

"I hope you know what you're doing," she said, her eyes pinning each one of them. "Tucker and Marty pulled these boys off the street, got them interested in something, helped them find a place in the community. Without this club, the boys are left to fend for themselves. Whatever happens now lies at your door."

She turned and walked out of the room, unable to say any more. Tears threatened, but she refused to shed them. Time enough for that later. She had to tell the boys.

Heart sinking, Ginny walked to the battered but still functional newspaper office. Once the building had been declared safe, Marty had insisted the boys keep meeting there, try to salvage what they could, even though he was unable to be with them. The boys had pitched in with a vengeance and helped his staff clean the place up and make it usable. Now they'd have to leave.

The group waited for her at the back, some sitting on the staff benches they'd painted yesterday, some standing.

"It's not good, is it?" Tom spoke for all of them.

"I'm sorry. The town council has insisted we disband."

They stared at each other in shock, eyes brimming with disappointment.

"But our plans!"

"Yeah. We were going to have a party for Tucker when he came back."

"And another one for Marty when he gets out of the hospital."

"I'm sorry." She didn't know what else to say. She'd tried so hard to find some proof of Tom's innocence. She'd questioned Vera several times, searched uselessly for something that would shift the blame. To no avail.

She'd failed Tucker.

Tucker. She closed her eyes, inhaled the soft evening air that carried only a faint reminder of the fire. Where was Tucker now?

"Ginny? Does that mean they'll be sending us back?"

She blinked at the gangly group of barely-teens clustered around her. "I'm afraid I don't know."

"They can't!"

The voice wasn't familiar. Ginny stretched to her tiptoes to see who'd spoken.

"They can't send us away." A lanky boy stomped forward. "They promised!"

"Well, now they're breaking that promise, Lane. You might as well get used to it." Nick shoved his hands in his pockets. "It always happens. We should have known."

"Yeah." Ira sneered at Lane. "You should be happy, man. The club's done, finished. Isn't that what you wanted?"

"No!" Lane's face blanched. "I never wanted that. I wanted to belong to it. To be a part of it. I didn't want to kill it." He stared at them, then flopped his head into his hands, his whole body slumped in dejection.

"Why do you care? I thought you hated us." Tom walked over to stand in front of the boy. "The last time we voted not to let you join, you said you didn't want to be part of it."

"I lied." Lane faced them all. He shook his head. "I wanted to be part of it so badly I could almost taste it."

He turned to face Ginny. "I never had friends, not real friends. I sure never had an airplane. Man, I wanted to see that plane fly."

"We all did, Lane. The boys had just collected enough money to buy the motor. We were going to launch it next week, when Marty came home." Ginny reached out to touch his knitted cap, trying to tell him how sorry she was. "I'm afraid it will never get off the ground now. The club is disbanded."

"Yeah, and all because some dumb people think Tom deliberately set that fire! As if." They started grumbling among themselves.

"The fire was my fault."

"Huh?"

"Say what?"

En masse the group turned to stare at the boy who'd tried numerous times to join their club.

"What do you mean, Lane?" Ginny positioned herself in front of him and sent a warning glance to the bigger boys, who looked ready to fight. "How could it possibly be your fault?"

"I didn't do it on purpose. Really I didn't."

"I believe you. Just tell us what happened, okay?" She felt a shiver of hope. Maybe Tucker's work wouldn't go down the drain. Maybe there was still a chance. "Go ahead. Take your time."

"I—well, that is, I guess you'd say I was jealous. I wanted to join so bad, but I didn't want anyone giving me rules." He glanced at the angry faces. "That's why I ran away from home in the first place. There were too many rules, all of them impossible to keep."

The boys never said a word, each waiting for the truth to emerge.

"I snuck in the back door that night. I was going to

hide until the meeting got started. I'd done it before. I came to every one and you guys didn't even know it." Aware of the glowers around him, Lane lost his grin.

"Next time maybe we'd better post a guard."

He'd been smoking right outside the door, and they hadn't even known. The match, Ginny remembered suddenly. The fire chief spoke of a match at the scene. Tucker knew it was a clue.

Ginny studied Lane's anguished face, knew he needed to confess. "Go on," she said quietly.

"If you guys didn't vote to let me belong to the club, I was going to do something to ruin your plans. I didn't know what, exactly. I was just mad."

"And then what happened?" Tom took over, his face grave as he watched the boy through narrowed eyes. "You were smoking, weren't you?"

"Yeah." Lane colored under their muttered condemnation. "I thought it was cool, smoking right under your noses. Then you guys split so I had to hide in the paper room. I waited, smoked a couple more, then I decided to scram. But Marty was there." Lane gulped. "Every time I started for the stairs, I'd hear him coming down. Then I didn't hear anything for a while. That's when I saw it."

Ginny almost smiled. Far from the punkish image he projected, Lane looked like nothing more than a frightened little boy.

"Saw what?"

"Smoke. It was coming from a pile of papers that were stacked there. I must have missed some matches."

"Or the ashes from your cigarette dropped onto it." Tom frowned at him. "That's why we have the rules, Lane. To stop stuff like that from happening. Anyway, you're too young to smoke."

"I know." The boy hung his head in shame.

"So you just took off?"

"No! I tried to put it out. I did. But there was too much paper, and it just got worse. Pretty soon I couldn't breathe. I rushed up the stairs and took off."

"You didn't think you should warn Marty?" Tom's hand reached out and grabbed one thin shoulder. "You didn't think you should warn him that you'd set his business on fire?"

Ginny could see he was furious, not for himself, but because of his foster father. She wanted to step in, but she sensed Tom needed to handle this himself. She waited.

"I thought he'd gone!" Lane stared at them, eyes huge in his white face. "I did. I called a couple of times, but no one answered me. So I ran away."

"But Mrs. Malloy insisted she saw Tom's red hair." Ginny frowned. "How could that be?" In one rush of understanding she noticed Lane's hat, his orange knitted cap. In the dark, in a flurry of fire and smoke, Vera Malloy had mistaken it for Tom's carrot top.

"My hat." He pulled it off. "I know I should have told someone, gone to the police or something." He begged them to understand. "But I didn't think they'd understand that it was an accident. I thought they'd put me in jail for hurting him." Tears welled as he gazed into Tom's face. "I sure didn't think they'd tie the whole thing to you. You're such a Goody Two-shoes, the leader and everything. I mean, how could they think it was you?"

Ginny nodded. How, indeed?

"I've done lots of mean things, lots of bad things. I even got punished for things I never did. I thought it would be okay, that things would work out. But then

when you said the club was closing, well—'' Lane stopped, tried to control the wobble in his voice. ''That club is the only thing I've ever cared about. It can't quit. It just can't!''

He turned to Ginny.

''I stopped smoking that night. Never even lit another match.'' His eyes met hers, compelling her to listen as he poured out his heart. ''I know I'll have to get punished. I know it's going to be hard, but couldn't you get your guy to give me a chance, to find me a special friend like these other guys have?''

''It's not that easy, Lane.'' Ginny wished she knew a way to deal with this. ''Marty's still in the hospital. It's going to be a while before he can come back to work. If ever.'' She stopped, let him absorb that. ''That fire did an awful lot of damage. I'm not sure how the police will feel.''

''But the other guy. What about him? Couldn't he help—talk to somebody or something?''

Her heart bumped against her ribs. Oh, how she wished Tucker could be here to see this, to witness the impact his work had on one young lonely boy.

''Tucker isn't available, Lane. He had to go out of town.''

''Oh.''

The disappointment in that one word stung her to action. She wouldn't give up. She'd promised Tucker to do her best and she would.

''So that leaves you and me, Lane. We'll just have to give it a try.'' She smiled, encouraged to see the hope return to his eyes. ''From here on it's complete honesty, no matter how badly it hurts. Okay?''

He nodded.

"All right." She took a deep breath. "You and I are going to take a trip over to the town council."

"We're coming." The boys, led by Tom, gathered behind her.

"It's our club, too. We want to know what happens."

Hadn't the whole thing started as a means to encourage them to take responsibility? She could hardly deny it now.

"All right, guys. You're on. Let's go."

Two days later Ginny sat on the deck with her father, watching the boy's club come to order. They'd been two of the longest days of her life, waiting, praying, hoping Tucker would soon come home.

"Tucker's going to be so proud of those boys." Adrian grinned, his healthy skin glowing in the last rays of the sun. "They do him credit."

"So do you. You didn't have to volunteer to hook Lane up with someone, you know. I could have done it."

His hand closed over hers, squeezed.

"I know, honey. But I wanted to do my part to keep things going. Just until he gets back. You understand?"

She nodded, tears welling in her eyes.

God had worked wonders in their small town. Tom had been completely exonerated. Lane was on probation but did not have to go to jail. Marty was out of the hospital, his lungs finally clear and his burns healing. His nephew has taken over the day-to-day operations until he started a new job in a few weeks. Marty would be able to collect his insurance and rebuild if he wanted. So many praises to give.

But the biggest miracle, Tucker's return, was still in the future.

Ginny refused to let on how worried she was. Every night, long after her father had retired, she pored over the late news, following the warring factions in a little-known African country. And every evening the news was worse. The fighting had escalated and the damage was horrific.

"I want to get this clubhouse finished so that when Tucker comes back, we can get busy on building another plane. Everybody agree?"

Ginny smiled. With Tom at the helm they had grown together, solidified into a unit that could not, would not be defeated.

"Okay, so let's get to work."

They sawed, hammered and nailed until the light was completely gone and the few flashlights Ginny had been able to scrounge were of no use.

The overcast sky shielded the moon, the rumbles in the west signaling a storm. At the first drop of rain, Ginny called a halt.

"I think you'd better stop now, Tom. I've seen a flash or two of lightning."

"Yeah, I saw it." He began putting the tools he'd borrowed from her father into their case. "It's getting closer with every one. Come on, you guys. We've got a curfew to keep."

Those words sent the others scurrying to clean up. A few moments later they were off, wishing her good-night one by one.

Only Tom remained.

She stood beside him, sheltered under the roof as the first drops began to fall. They waited together as the storm intensified and the rain came down in sheets.

"Do you think he's all right?" The words seemed to be dragged out of him almost against his will.

"I think Tucker's in God's hands. That's the safest place he can be."

"I know."

It was clear to Ginny that Tom's mind wasn't at peace. She waited, hoping he'd tell her what was bothering him.

"It's just that I thought maybe we'd hear something. You know? Maybe a news report that he was there covering a story. Something."

"Me, too." Ginny wrapped her arm around him in a consoling hug.

A jagged spear of white light slashed across the sky, illuminating the clubhouse for a few seconds.

"He loves you." Tom glanced at her, his eyes dark, thoughtful. "I'm no expert, of course. Until I came here, I didn't even know what love was. I thought it was like in the movies."

"And now you don't?"

He shook his head.

"Love is something you can see in action." Tom's forehead pleated in thought. "It's like when Tucker tells us we have to make sure and thank you for the goodies or invite you to our stuff."

He eased out from under her arm. Ginny grinned. He was as normal as any other teenage boy. He didn't want a girl hugging him in public, but he didn't want to hurt her feelings, either. It was touching.

"It's not just because he's teaching us manners and stuff. It's more because he wants to make sure you know we appreciate you, that we want to include you. He doesn't want you to be left out. Tucker cares about you and your feelings."

Ginny couldn't stop the tears from welling. She longed so much for Tucker to love her. Could Tom be

right? Was it possible that he really did feel more for her than the caring he'd talked about?

"He asked me to look out for you and your dad while he was gone."

The words shocked her.

"He did?"

"Uh-huh. After he told me the truth about his friend's death." Tom's face suffused a bright red. "He said I should make sure you didn't do too much, that sometimes when you were worried you tried to fix things and overdid it. You won't, will you? Tucker wouldn't like it."

He looked so anxious that Ginny could do little else but agree.

"I promise I'll call you if I need anything. But I think right now we'd better call Marty and ask him if you can stay here for tonight. I don't think it's a good idea to go out in this storm."

He gave her a serious look, then nodded.

"I'll call him."

Ginny stayed on the deck while he phoned, enjoying the fresh scent of rain that cooled off the day.

"I think she's lonely, Marty," Tom whispered. "She asked me to stay tonight. If it's okay with you, I'd like to. Tucker told me to be available."

Ginny smiled at the quiet words. Dear Tucker. About to go off to the one place he feared most, to enter the same situation he'd barely escaped from, and he'd thought of her.

Wasn't that love?

Chapter Fourteen

Ginny loved Sunday afternoons, especially warm sunny ones. She'd changed after church, left her father napping upstairs and come down to putter in her flower garden.

Tucker had been gone for days, and she'd still not heard a word. Why was it taking so long?

She'd run out of words to pray. God knew her heart. All she could do was keep petitioning Him for Tucker's safety.

She gathered a bouquet of iris, lilies, dianthus and bachelor's buttons. They'd look perfect on the foyer table for tonight's service.

She checked on her father, scribbled a note, then hurried down the street. It felt good to stretch her legs, to work off some of the tension that had been growing over the past few days.

The church was empty, which was too bad because sunbeams streamed through the windows and lit the cross at the front. Ginny sat in a pew, a sense of holy awe surrounding her.

Her heart lifted, danced upward like the dust motes caught in the beams of light.

Tucker's face swam into her mind.

Keep the faith, Gin. For me. Once more she felt the touch of his lips on hers. *I will be back. I promise. Don't you forget it.*

The door of the church opened. Ginny turned, smiled when she saw Tom step inside. He always seemed in awe of the sanctuary, as if there was something to be afraid of in here.

"Hi, Tom. I brought some flowers and sat down to think."

He stepped forward gingerly. Once he came closer Ginny caught a glimpse of his face. He was upset.

"Tom?"

He sat beside her, gathered her hands into his. His fingers were icy cold, and the chill from them rippled up her nerves, clenching her heart.

"What's wrong? Is it Dad?"

"No." He shook his red head. "Your father is fine. I just saw him. But I think you should go be with him, Ginny."

She frowned. "Why? What's wrong?"

Tears welled in his sad eyes. His chin wobbled.

"He's dead, Ginny. Tucker's dead."

"No!" She jerked back, dragged her hands from his, surging to her feet. "I don't believe you."

Tom nodded. "It's true."

"It can't be. Not now." *The promise, God. What about the promise?*

"I was at your place. Your dad had the radio on. We were talking." He stopped, gulped, then plunged on. "A news report came on." He shook his head, tears welling in his eyes. "They said he'd been killed. Tucker's dead."

She sat slowly, her legs crumpling.

"Why?" she whispered. "Why?" She lifted her head, searching Tom's face. "He was coming back," she told him. "He promised he'd come back."

"I know." Gingerly he reached out and took her hand. "Come on, Ginny. Let's go home."

She did what he said, put one foot in front of the other until she was climbing the front steps of her home.

Her father wrapped her in a tight embrace, but Ginny couldn't respond. She felt frozen, numbed.

"He's God, honey. He knows what He's doing."

She stared at him, tears coursing down her cheeks in a steady river.

"You have to trust Him, Ginny. All things work together, remember? For good."

She couldn't listen to it, couldn't hear those words right now. She reached out one finger to touch the full-blown petals of Tucker's roses, then lifted one flower out and buried her face in its scent.

"I need to be alone for a while. Okay?" She didn't wait for an answer, but walked through the house.

The yard was just as sunny, the flowers just as beautiful, but none of it touched her soul now.

She caught sight of the clubhouse and automatically walked to the base of it. She climbed slowly, knowing this was where she needed to be. She felt close to Tucker here.

The tears came then, hot, aching tears of bitter regret. They fell unheeded as she begged for an answer.

"Why? Why did he have to go?"

The answer stole into her heart in a still, soft voice.

Am I truly Lord? Are you willing to deny your will and trust that I want only the best for you?

The truth flooded into her mind. God's will—that's what she'd been trying to deny. She'd been working overtime to make her desires God's. She hadn't truly submitted to letting Him control her future.

She acknowledged it with a soft sigh of repentance.

"I'm sorry. Your way is always best." The pain was almost unbearable, but in her heart, in her soul, she kissed Tucker goodbye.

"Whatever You want, Lord, that's what I'll do."

The pain didn't leave, but a soft, sweet peace stole into her heart. God was in control. He would help her deal with Tucker's death. He would make something good come out of it.

As she glanced around the clubhouse, Ginny realized that something good already had. The boys were stronger now. They still needed a leader, and she would put her heart and soul into finding one for them, someone who would challenge them as Tucker had. They would be fine. Something good had come from his short time here.

She looked at the rose still clutched in her fingers.

"I love you, Tucker."

"I love you, too, Gin. I always have."

She let the dream continue until a hand closed over her shoulder. Then she twisted to smile at Tom and saw instead Tucker's beloved face.

"I really do love you. I didn't understand that until I was driving away that night. I love you more than anything else in my life." He gathered her still body into his arms and kissed her with a tenderness that said more than any words.

"Tucker?" Ginny touched his cheek, his eyes, his hair. "Is it really you?"

"It's me."

He smiled, and it was her undoing. She wrapped her arms around him, sobbing with joy, relief and praises to God, who'd swiftly given back what she'd taken months to surrender.

He held her face between his palms, fingers threading through her hair as he examined every feature.

"I'm a fool, Gin. An idiot. I couldn't see it, couldn't understand it, when all the time you were right there looking me in the face. It took leaving to see the truth and hunkering down in a soggy foxhole to realize that I wanted it back, all of it."

She couldn't get over his return.

"But how did it happen? How did you get out?"

"Your dad and Tom are the only two other people who know I'm alive. It was part of the deal I made so I could get that rookie out."

"A deal with Ulysses?" She laid her head on his chest, content to listen forever if it meant they could be together.

"He and his buddies. They wanted the truth of the story told to correct the impression the other side have given the United Nations."

"And you told it?" She frowned. "We didn't hear anything."

"You will. Tomorrow. I'll have a report on the air at six a.m. giving news of a military coup in an African country that's recently been torn apart by war." He lifted her head, staring into her eyes. "It's the last newscast I'll make, Gin."

"The last?" She frowned. "Tucker, you love your work. You can't quit!"

"I love you more, Gin. Besides, I want to come home. I've run around the world long enough."

"Home? To the Junction, you mean?" She didn't understand what he was saying, what he was trying to tell her. "Why?"

"It's going to take me a few minutes to explain."

"I'm here."

"I know." He kissed the top of her head, then sprawled on the floor of the clubhouse, his back against the rough, splintered logs, Ginny snuggled in his arms.

"I figured something out. It took being sent back to that hell for me to understand that Quint's death and my injuries were God's wake-up call."

She snuggled closer, eyes closed as she listened to his dear voice.

"I sat there with guns blasting all around me, waiting for them to negotiate with the network for our lives. That's when I realized that in the scheme of things, my presence on this earth, even being allowed to be here, is a gift."

He tilted her chin. Ginny opened her eyes and saw the sheer on joy in his.

"I wasn't there because of some freak of nature, Ginny. I was there because God couldn't get my attention any other way. The doubts were a way of confronting my past and growing beyond that. He had a new plan for me, a new vision. But I was so mired in the ugliness I saw every day I couldn't get beyond that to see the future. Quint's death was the start of my wake-up call."

"But how—" She frowned, trying to fathom it.

"I went down my own path for a long time, Gin. That's how I got so alienated from God. I saw success, fame, money, and I started to believe that all those things were mine, if only I could prove myself. The last seven years have been about me."

Ginny didn't understand what he was saying. Tucker smiled, the pad of his thumb gentle against her jaw.

"I wanted the best from life, and what I saw was the worst—but it wasn't a mistake. I see that now. It was all part of the plan."

"The plan?"

He chuckled at her confusion.

"Uh-huh. The plan. God's plan. A plan to give me what I really wanted all along."

"Which is?" She shifted, tired of being kept in suspense. "If you're not going back to reporting, what are you going to do?"

"I thought I'd stay here, marry you and run the paper."

Ginny stared at him, her heart thumping at three times its normal pace. Could it be? Could it really be that her dream would at last come true?

"I know how ugly the world is, Gin. I've seen it firsthand, and I've told the world what I saw. But now I want to do something about it. Tom told me about Lane. He's like a different kid." Tucker squeezed her hand in his, his eyes blazing with purpose.

"I've seen the difference a little time and attention can make in the boys' lives. I believe the paper could do the same thing, that I could use it as a vehicle to reach this community and beyond."

Suddenly she got it. Having seen the worst, God had also shown Tucker the possibilities of the best.

"I want to be part of the solution, Ginny. A means by which people can experience joy, good news instead of ugliness, hope instead of despair. I want to show people God's love can carry them through anything. It's one way to stop hate from taking over here. And if we stop it here, we can stop it anywhere.''

Before her very eyes, as he spoke from his heart, Tucker's vision grew in vibrant strength and wonder.

''If we start with the people in the Junction, start letting go of anger and hate and begin to see each other as friends and learn to understand in this corner, maybe we can make a dent in world peace.'' He frowned. ''Of course, I'm not sure if Marty will want to sell out to me, but I know he often spoke of retiring. Maybe he'll want to stay on.''

''The details don't really matter, though, do they, Tuck?'' she whispered. ''The Father has all of that worked out.''

He nodded, his fingers threading through her curls.

''I'm only just beginning to understand that,'' he said. ''If we let go and let God, anything can happen. Look at us.''

Ginny refused to cry. Not now. Not when the Lord had just handed her the desire of her heart.

''Yes, look at us,'' she agreed with a tremulous smile. ''Seven years, and you're finally going to keep your promise.''

He blushed. The sight of it made Ginny giggle. He dropped his chin on her head and hugged her closer.

''I guess I needed some work done on my heart before I could finally keep my word.''

With tender strength Tucker turned her in his arms.

''I love you, Ginny Brown. I want to marry you and get started on this wonderful new life. How long do I have to wait?''

''Two weeks?''

He grinned.

"Perfect. I'll meet you at the church in two weeks. And then we're never going to be parted again."

Ginny didn't respond. She couldn't. She was too busy kissing him.

After a few moments, Tucker lifted his head and deliberately searched out her feet.

"You promised to get a new pair of shoes for my return," he teased.

Ginny nodded. She lifted one hand to touch his beloved face. "How about if I wear something special to our wedding?"

His eyes teased her.

"I can hardly wait."

The church was full. The entire town had turned out to see Ginny Brown finally marry Tucker Townsend. Folks in Jubilee Junction said it was the longest engagement ever.

Ginny didn't care. Her dream was finally coming true. What difference did a few years make?

She peeked out the door one more time. Tucker still had not appeared at the front of the church, and he was five minutes late. Where was he?

"He'll be here, honey. You know that." Adrian smoothed her veil away from her face, his eyes shining with love.

"I know. It's just—"

"Okay, Ginny. We're ready now." Tom grinned at her, a completely new Tom dressed in a tux, his hair slicked back. "We finally got the groom here, but it took some doing." He saw her glance at the front of the church. "Everything okay?"

"Everything's wonderful. I'm just a little nervous, I

guess.'' Ginny wiped a tear from the corner of her eye and huffed a sigh of relief.

"Well, get over it! I put a lot of work into this wedding and I'd like to see it through.''

A bubble of laughter burst out, barely smothered as her father led her toward the aisle.

"Don't worry, Tom. I'm not backing out.''

"Thank goodness!'' He scurried away.

Tom's work would not go unnoticed by anyone today. The boys lined the aisle of the church, dressed in rented tuxedos that matched Tom's, right down to the pale pink roses in their lapels and darker pink cummerbunds.

Ginny clutched her bouquet a little tighter, firmed her grip on her father's arm and looked straight ahead, her eyes finding Tucker at last. Why was he late? Was he having second thoughts?

One glance at his face assured her that Tucker Townsend knew exactly what he was doing. She could see the love blazing out at her. Then his eyes slid down the silken cloud of her dress to her feet, a question in their depths.

Ginny lifted her skirt just a bit and let him see the flimsy blue satin sandals with their skinny heels and tiny straps. She'd chosen them especially for this day.

His eyes slid up, met hers, a glint in their depths.

"Don't fall,'' he mouthed.

She rolled her eyes. "I won't.''

"Come on, then.'' He nodded his approval, then smiled at her, a grin so chock full of love she couldn't be nervous.

Ginny stepped forward, then stopped, surprised, when the boys tossed rose petals onto the carpet in front of her. Whose idea was that?

Tom winked.

"Plucking these things takes a lot of time," he whispered. "Tucker spent the morning driving to the city so we'd have enough. I'm afraid we made him late. Sorry, Ginny, but we wanted everything perfect."

Heart bursting, she leaned over to kiss him on the cheek.

"It is. Absolutely perfect. Thank you, guys." She included them all in her smile.

Then, with her father's arm supporting her, Ginny walked down the aisle to Tucker.

The service was short. That was Tucker's choice. His only break with convention was the little speech he offered her before he gave her a ring.

"Ginny, you are the most beautiful woman I've ever known." His voice was strong, firm and yet so tender. "Inside and out, you radiate God's love. It took me a long time to let that love inside, to let its light heal the hurts and show me a better way."

He pulled something out of his pocket.

"I once told you I didn't believe in happily ever after." His voice dropped so the congregation had to lean forward to hear. "You are my happily ever after, Gin, my hope for the future."

He slipped a magnificent diamond ring onto her finger. Ginny stared as the sunlight caught the facets and shimmered a blaze of light. It was a glorious ring, but it couldn't surpass the rich glow of love on his face.

Tucker bent his head and kissed her hand, but he didn't release it. Ginny held her breath as he spoke again, his voice so soft only she could hear.

"I'm giving you this ring as my pledge. I will love and cherish you forever. You've lived in my heart for more than seven years, Gin. You belong there." And then he slipped a wide gold band into place, guarding the diamond.

She wasn't supposed to say anything. She hadn't planned a speech. But somehow, as she repeated the vows the pastor recited, the words slid into her mind, and she knew she had to say them.

"Loving you was worth the wait, Tucker. I'm giving you this ring as a promise that whereever you go, whatever you do, I will always believe in you."

She slid the ring onto his finger.

"I love you."

"Tucker, you may kiss your bride."

His kiss was filled with promise, but it was far too short. Ginny didn't protest. She turned with him to face the folks of Jubilee Junction as the announcement was made.

"Ladies and gentlemen, may I present Tucker and Ginny Townsend."

They walked down the aisle under a canopy of confetti, which the boys delightedly tossed over them. Outside, friends and relatives gathered around to congratulate the happy couple.

Marty limped up, grabbed Tucker's hand and pumped it vigorously. "Congratulations. I'm already feeling lots better."

Coach Bains stepped up, whacked Tucker on the back, a huge grin lighting his face.

"Took you long enough. In my day, we worked a little faster."

Marty grinned. The boys hooted.

Tucker ignored their gibes. He dusted the confetti off his shoulders, then clasped Ginny's hand in his.

"Good things come to those who wait, Gin," he

whispered. "I promised you happily ever after, and you're going to get it."

"Something tells me it's not going to take you seven years to keep this promise." She grinned.

He bent to brush his lips over hers.

"The rest of my life, Gin. That's how long it's gonna take to finish this story."

She snuggled into the arm he wrapped around her waist.

"Okay."

She was Tucker's bride. She could wait for whatever else God had in store.

* * * * *

Hello!

Nice to see you again. I hope you've enjoyed Tucker and Ginny's story. Much of what they learned in their faith walk has been gleaned from my own life and the needless fussing and fuming I've done when life throws me a curveball I hadn't expected and don't know how to handle.

But you know, valleys look so beautiful when you view them from a distance. Maybe we need to wait a bit before we decide this particular trial is too terrible to bear. Maybe it will lead to tremendous joy or a new lesson about God. Remember, the only way to get to the mountaintop is to go through that valley, whether it lasts seven years, like Ginny's, or seven days.

I pray you'll truly find the peace that God imparts as He strengthens you, and then works out all things together for your good.

Blessings,